"GIVE US A SIGN..."

THE CHANDELIER CRYSTALS CLINKED as it shook. A glass clattered against a tray on the far side of the room. A chair moved as it if had been bumped and suddenly Elizabeth felt something ice cold pass through her. She must have gasped because Simon clenched her hand in his and was looking at her with concern.

"I felt her," Mary cried. "She passed right through me!"

"She seems upset," Madame Petrovka said. "How did she die?"

Graham answered in a hushed and hoarse voice. "Drowned. She was just four."

"Sometimes spirits, especially the young, don't understand what's happened to them," Madame Petrovka said. "Are you afraid to cross over, child?"

She appeared to be listening to a voice only she heard. "What's wrong, child?"

She listened again and her face grew grim. "Everyone must remain calm no matter what should happen next..."

The **Out of Time** Series
by Monique Martin

Out of Time

When the Walls Fell

Please check Monique's website,
http://moniquemartin.weebly.com/
for news of new and upcoming books!

MONIQUE MARTIN

when the Walls Fell

Out of Time Series
Book 2

FOR MORE INFORMATION, PLEASE contact writtenbymonique@gmail.com.

COVER PHOTO: KAREN WUNDERMAN
COVER LAYOUT AND INTERIOR formatting by: TERyvisions

ISBN 10: 1467957984
ISBN 13: 978-1467957984

FIRST PAPERBACK EDITION

Acknowledgements

This book would not have been possible without the help and support of many people: Robin, who's been there since before the beginning and has custody of half my brain. Sandy, Michael, KC, LK, and Vicki for helping me make good better, Terry for her wonderful work on the cover, My mom, George, Edd & Carole for their encouragement and support. Greg from The Winkley Company for his generosity and kindness. And my dad for being there every step of the way.

I'd also like to thank the thousands of people who help preserve the past through books, websites, museums and sheer will.

When the Walls Fell

Monique Martin

Prologue

London, 1900

A DEEP, RED SMILE OF blood oozed from the gash at the guard's temple. She raised the manacles over her head, ready to strike him again. The iron was heavy and sure.

Through the screams, she heard noises down the corridor. She looked down at the guard as he lay on the cold hospital floor. His eyes had rolled back in his head. His arm stuck out in front of him, frozen in a moment of fear. If it had been Nurse Fletcher instead of the guard, she would have swung again. And again. And again.

That was the one part of the plan she didn't like, but he'd been right. She wanted to be the one to kill Fletcher, but if she'd had the chance, she would have gladly forsaken freedom to savor the sweetness of that revenge. At least this way, Nurse Fletcher would be just as dead; he'd promised that, and she would be free. Free to do what she'd spent the last decade dreaming of. Outside these walls a sweeter vengeance waited.

3

Heavy footfalls echoed down the hall. The other guards were coming. She stepped over the body of the dead guard and took the large ring from his belt. Dozens of keys slipped around the metal, but she knew what she was looking for.

She turned the lock and opened the heavy door. Cold, sooty London air bit through the thin material of her gown, but she felt only freedom. She tossed the key ring onto the guard's body and ran. She ran into the shadows of night. She ran barefoot across the wet grass and cold gravel. She ran toward freedom.

Dogs barked in the distance. They'd gone to the kennel. She had to hurry.

She flattened herself along the thick, stone wall of her prison. The barking grew louder, closer.

A large horse-drawn carriage moved past on the street just outside the gate. She knew this was her only chance. She ran toward the back of the carriage, but she bumped into someone, something. She didn't dare look back. She grabbed on to the carriage and pulled herself onto the small ledge. She curled up inside the luggage box and pulled the black fabric flap down to cover her. The carriage rolled down the street and into the heart of London.

The dogs would lose her scent. She was free.

And he was going to pay.

CHAPTER ONE

THE SUN PEEKED THROUGH the sheers as unwanted as the morning. Simon had woken Elizabeth in the cool grays of predawn light to make love before the rest of the world stirred to life. He'd been dreading this day, and not just because the private bliss of holiday was soon to be overrun with fatuous students and soporific lectures, although that was reason enough. He'd greedily savored their time alone where they could live cloistered from the world, where her smile was only for him.

He was a selfish bastard really, he thought as he gazed down at her still wrapped in dreams. The morning light caressed her cheek and like a jealous lover, he raised his hand to block the sun. The shadow of his fingers traced the contours of her face. As if she could feel his ghostly touch, she nuzzled closer to his body. Simon closed his eyes and pulled Elizabeth more securely into his embrace. The day could wait a little longer.

Time, tide and the new winter quarter wait for no man, and the alarm clock finally sounded. With a swift movement Simon silenced the painful country western music station Elizabeth insisted they set the damnable thing to. He mumbled something rather rude about the singer's wife-cousin and dog, Chet under his breath and dropped his head back onto the pillow.

Elizabeth gave a husky laugh that did nothing to further Simon's desire to get out of bed.

"You have a decidedly twisted sense of humor," he said, hoping to steal a few more minutes next to her sleep-warmed skin.

"That's why you love me," Elizabeth said, giving him a quick kiss.

"In spite of that." He caught her and pulled her into his arms. "In definite spite."

After a long, far from sufficiently satisfying kiss,

Elizabeth eased back and arched an eyebrow. "Why Professor Cross, I think you're stalling."

Simon tried to frown, but she was right. He was due at University for pre-term office hours, which, to his mind, were a complete waste of time. It was an odd sensation, this sudden urge to shirk his responsibilities. Although, he hadn't exactly embraced many of his professorial duties, he'd never wanted to toss them aside for more pleasurable pursuits. Then again, he thought as he looked down at the woman in his bed, he'd never had such a pleasure to pursue before. He shook his head in defeat and pulled back the covers. "All right, Miss West, up with you then."

She clutched at the quickly receding blanket. "But it's cold."

"If I have to suffer, you have to suffer."

She huffed out her breath in dramatic indignation. "You're very Simon Legree today."

He chuckled and tossed her robe. "Come along, Cassy."

"Very funny." She put it on and tied the sash. "I almost forgot. Can you give me a lift to the mechanic's? My car should be ready today."

Simon shrugged on his dressing gown. "I don't see why you insist on throwing good money after bad."

"It's a classic," Elizabeth said as she started for the bathroom.

Simon followed closely behind. "It's a bloody death trap."

Elizabeth splashed water onto her face. "But a classic death trap."

He handed her a towel and glared at her reflection in the mirror. Why was she so intransigent? "Elizabeth, I really wish you'd let me buy you another car."

Her expression was lost in the towel, but he could hear the frown in her voice. "Haven't we had this conversation before?"

"I live with irrational hope that someday you'll be rational about it."

She handed him the soggy towel and slipped past him to turn on the shower taps.

"I don't see why you won't let me give you something that's well within my means to give. Not to mention the fact that I wouldn't have to wonder if you survived each trip to university."

She stared into the shower for a moment before answering. Her voice was so soft he barely heard it above the running water. "Because it's mine."

They'd been down this path before and he still had yet to fully comprehend her reservations. "What I have *is* yours."

"I know that," she said as she turned to face him. "And I appreciate it, but it's…"

Simon sighed and finished her sentence for her. "The first and only thing that's ever truly been yours."

He knew how little she'd had and how much the little she did have meant to her. He simply could not understand why she balked at his attempts to give her more. He would give her the earth and everything on it if she asked. Stepping forward, he wrapped his arms about her waist.

She seemed ready to give some very pithy response, but merely ducked her head briefly in temporary defeat and gave him a fleeting kiss before stepping into the shower.

Simon watched the glass door close between them. Perhaps it was the way her lips brushed against his, or the sixth sense a lover has for his partner, but Simon knew that something else was wrong. With the practiced and stalwart nature of a man long on the short end of things, his chest tightened and he pretended not to notice.

In the nearly four months since their return from 1929 New York City, Simon had grappled with the changes in his life—from exclusive to inclusive, from the periphery to a center he was sure could not hold.

An accident with his grandfather's pocket watch had thrown them both back in time to Prohibition era New York. He'd fought his attraction to Elizabeth for as long as he could. But the arrival of a gangster, intent on having Elizabeth for his own, lit a fire under the coals that had been his heart. As a professor of the Occult, he'd found the proof he'd been searching for, and as a man he'd found the love the he'd been hiding from. He'd nearly lost her and vowed he'd do anything to keep that from happening again. The rest of the world be damned.

The first few days after their return were a blur of pain and the ecstasy of being alive, of being together. The physical wounds had healed in their course. Elizabeth still had the fading remnants of a scar on her forehead from the boat's explosion. The soft pink crescent mark was the only visible sign of what they'd endured. There were scars that weren't so easily healed or seen.

"Are you all right?" she asked, breaking him from his reverie.

With his thumb he brushed a wet strand of hair from her cheek and nodded.

She leaned into his touch. "I think about it too."

He smiled wanly. Her memories, despite it all, were fond remembrances of how their life together had begun. His were painful recollections of how it had almost ended.

She tipped her head up and kissed the corner of his mouth, just as she had for their first kiss, months, decades ago. This time, he didn't pull away, afraid to love her. This time, he held her tightly, afraid to let go.

Simon was already sitting at a table when Elizabeth arrived at the restaurant for lunch. "Sorry, I'm late. Meeting ran over."

"Everything all right?" he asked as he rose and pulled out her chair.

His instinctive manners were one of the many things she loved about him. Sometimes he was too good to be true—green eyes the color of Absinthe, a long, lean body that moved with easy grace and a baritone voice with a cut glass British accent.

He took his seat again. "Your car didn't break down again, did it?"

He was also a royal pain. She spread her napkin out across her lap. "My car is just fine. Thank you for asking."

"I was only joking, Elizabeth," he said and reached across the table to take her hand.

Just when she was all ready to get riled up, he had to go and be charming. Her buttons were far too easily pushed these days. One innocent question from him and she was ready to jump down his throat. Not that she didn't adore him even when he was being a pill. He meant well, but ever since they'd come back he'd been her constant shadow. At first, she loved the feeling of absolute safety his omnipresence had provided. Who didn't want to be loved to distraction? Until it became…distracting.

After the first few months what had been cocooning became smothering. She didn't blame him. She could only imagine what it must have been like for him after she'd disappeared. Mostly because he hadn't actually told her what he'd gone through.

"I wish they hadn't let Louis go," Simon said. "The menu has never been the same."

"The Vichy just doesn't soise like it used to."

"Very droll." Simon peered over the edge of his menu and narrowed his eyes. "Something is wrong."

"No, nothing's wrong," she said and bit the inside of her cheek in penance for the lie. Not that anything was really wrong, though she doubted Simon would see it that way.

Simon wasn't a big fan of change and while she was certain this one was for the best, she knew he was going to resist every step of the way. She also knew she had to spit out the truth sooner or later. Unfortunately, later was catching up with her, but she wasn't finished stalling quite yet. "How was your morning? Any students dare to enter the inner sanctum?"

He closed his menu and set it aside. "As a matter of fact. I'm afraid you may have to have one of your talks with Mr. Goode."

"I knew I should have glued that hourglass to your desk."

Simon smirked in response and continued, "He had the ludicrous notion that I was in need of a new assistant."

Elizabeth nearly choked. Damn the campus gossip grapevine. It was worse than a beauty parlor. "He did?"

"Someone's idea of joke, I suppose."

Later was now. "Or not," she said softly.

"I'm sorry?"

She took a deep breath and plunged ahead. "Nothing's official yet, but I have been thinking about talking to Professor Aumond about working as his assistant. Or maybe even looking for something outside of the university."

Simon looked as if he'd been slapped. He jerked his head back and blinked several times before he muttered, "You what?"

The shock in his voice took her breath away for a moment. He wasn't angry; he was hurt. "I know I should have said something

sooner, but I wanted to think about it first. Nothing's set. I'm...
I'm just thinking about it."

He leaned back in his chair dumbstruck. They sat in silence as
a ten months pregnant elephantine pause stretched out between
them. When he finally spoke, his voice was flat. "How long have
you been planning on leaving me?"

The guilt that had taken up residence in her heart at the start
of the conversation just sublet a room to shame. She wasn't leaving. There was no planning. There was a definite lack of planning
involved here. Maybe there should have been more planning. She
fiddled with her napkin. This wasn't going well at all.

"I'm not. I'm just thinking about the future."

"I see."

No, he didn't see. Couldn't see. She loved being his assistant,
but she wanted more than that. She wanted to be his partner, but
as long as he was signing her timecard that wasn't going to happen.
Not to mention that a few members of the university board had
raised eyebrows and pursed lips at her and Simon's work and home
hybrid relationship.

She reminded herself that being in a relationship was new territory for Simon. He'd managed to live his life without getting
close to anyone and now that he was, it made him feel raw and
vulnerable. For a man used to very firm footing, this was like a
tightrope act without a net.

"Simon, I love you. I'm just thinking about taking another job
is all. And I'm just thinking about it. It might be best for both of
us. But nothing's changed yet."

He ran his finger up and down the stem of his water glass. "Was
there something about our...arrangement that bothered you?"

"Aside from you calling it an arrangement?" she said in an
attempt to leaven the situation, but it fell matzo flat on the table
between them. "I love being with you, working with you, but we
can't do both."

"I don't see why they're mutually exclusive."

"The Board does."

"I don't give a bloody good damn what the Board thinks," Simon said loudly, causing people at nearby tables to turn and glare their disapproval.

"But I do," she said quietly. "You deserve their respect and as long you're sleeping with your assistant, an ex-student, you'll never get it."

"Then I'll quit."

"And give up teaching? You bark about it, but I know how much you love it. You don't have to work, but you do. Nobody does that unless they love it."

"You didn't have to go behind my back."

She huffed out a breath and tried to keep a cool head. Why did growing pains have to be so painful? "I didn't go anywhere. And it's not just the board, although that's reason enough. I can't stay your assistant forever. I just think it might be for the best."

"For the best?"

"Why are you making this so hard?"

"I'm sorry, am I forgetting to play my part?"

Elizabeth gripped her napkin tightly in a fist. "That's not fair."

"I dare you to find anything about this situation that is."

Elizabeth took a deep breath and let it out slowly. "I know this is a shock." Simon snorted, but she kept on. "I know I probably should have discussed this with you sooner."

"Is that what we're doing? Discussing it? If that's the case then let me give you my opinion. You'd be a fool to work for Aumond."

She counted to ten before she responded. "I understand that you have issues with him, but—"

Simon crossed his arms over his chest. "This has nothing to do with me."

"Doesn't it? You're angry because I didn't tell you what I was thinking and the reason I didn't is because you'd be angry."

He slammed his palms down on the table causing the water glass to nearly topple over. "And shouldn't I be?"

"No. That's just it, Simon. You might, oh I don't know, consider what I want."

"Don't I always?"

"No," she said with forced equanimity, the sort she knew got under his skin. "You consider what *you* want me to have."

She could tell that had hit mark. His expression faltered before he got all British again. "Forgive me for looking out for your welfare."

"I did manage to get up in the morning and make it through the day before I met you."

As soon as she'd said it, she wished she could grab the words and cram them back down her throat. Simon's mask of control dropped for the barest of seconds and she saw the vulnerability behind it. His jaw muscles flexed under the strain of keeping his composure.

"Simon—"

"You made yourself perfectly clear," he said as he placed his napkin on the table.

"Simon—"

He shook his head and stood. Taking out his wallet, he pitched a few bills onto the table. "I'm sure you can manage perfectly well."

MONIQUE MARTIN

CHAPTER TWO

ELIZABETH SQUEEZED HER CAR into a tiny parking space under a leaky pipe and yanked up the emergency brake. Her VW Beetle groaned and creaked in protest, but she didn't care. God, she'd made a mess of things. She wanted to go to Simon's, but had no idea what to say. She shouldn't have waited so long to discuss it with him. She'd seriously taken the chicken exit on that one, but now it was done. There was nothing left to do but give him some time.

She rummaged in her purse and found her keys. She hadn't been back to her apartment in weeks. The plants she hadn't already managed to kill were probably dead by now. Three ferns and one relationship, not bad for a day's work. The door to her apartment always stuck and so she pressed her shoulder against it and gave it a good shove. It flew open, and she stumbled unceremoniously into her pitiful, little bachelorette.

She closed the door, tossed her purse onto the Goodwill couch, and headed straight for the kitchenette. Everything in the apartment was an ette. The refrigerator was squat and older than she was, but blissfully still cold. She opened the door and pulled out an open bottle of chardonnay, yanked the cork and sniffed. Not too skunky considering it had been there for weeks. She poured herself a glass and took a deep swig.

Sour grapes. She swallowed the irony with the wine. Her little apartment had never seemed so little before. Damn Simon and his spacious living.

As she looked around, everything about her place spoke of someone living somewhere else. Clothes were strewn about in the haste of packing and not caring what she left behind. A washed bra, long forgotten, still hung on the partition she'd jury-rigged to create a bedroom space. It was her apartment and not even a crackerjack size, but it had never felt confining before. Until now.

She poured the rest of the wine down the water-stained sink and walked back into the living room area. Maybe Simon had called, but the ancient answering machine's red light stared back dull and unblinking. Even her cell phone had nothing to say.

Maybe she deserved a little silent treatment. She'd really bungled this one. She'd wanted him to see her as a partner, so she'd gone behind his back. Smooth.

She could still see Simon's face when she'd said she could manage without him. If there'd been a ref there, she definitely would have had a point deducted for a low blow.

Worst yet, she knew better. Not that she was any Dr. Phil, but she knew how hard this was for Simon. For him, being with someone was like being suddenly left-handed. It was awkward and sometimes you jabbed yourself in the nose when you brushed your teeth.

Sighing, she plopped down onto the couch. The lump she'd nicknamed "Sciatica" dug into her hip. The scarf hanging on the wall as a poor man's version of tapestry drooped at one corner, the thumbtack lying in wait for her bare foot. This was home.

Closing her eyes, she listened for the familiar muffled sounds of apartment life, but everything was eerily silent. A knock at the door interrupted her start of her pity party. Elizabeth jerked upright and breathed out a sigh of relief. Simon. They'd argue a little more, talk it out, and have crazy monkey make-up sex. All in all, not so bad.

She walked over to the door and pushed out a cleansing breath before opening it. "Simon, I—"

A slight, balding man in a rumpled suit stared back at her with nervous, bright eyes behind black-rimmed glasses. He was the sort of man who was, even in his early forties, the spitting image of the boy he'd been. As he shifted his briefcase from the tight, clutching grip against his chest and into one hand, he offered her the other. "Miss West, it's… it's an honor to meet you."

Elizabeth took a cautious step backward and gripped the edge of the door. "And you are?"

"Oh, I'm sorry. Peter Travers," he said in a thin, high-pitched voice that sounded a little like Piglet and then glanced anxiously around the hallway where fluorescent lights flickered with a will of their own. "Could we continue this inside? I…I'd feel much better inside."

"I'm sure you would, but I'm afraid I'm just not interested in whatever it is you're selling," she said, gesturing to his briefcase.

"Oh, I'm not a salesman," he said and then squared his slender shoulders and lowered his voice. "I'm with the Council. The Council for Temporal Studies."

Elizabeth's grip on the edge of the door tightened. "The… the Council?" Horrible thoughts that she'd somehow single-handedly mangled the space-time continuum flooded her mind. "What do you want with me?"

"I'd rather discuss this inside. If that's all right with you?" A door opened and slammed down the hall causing him to jump so badly he had to right his glasses. He fished a handkerchief out of his pocket and mopped his shiny forehead. "Please?"

"Right," Elizabeth said, her mind still spinning, and allowed him into the apartment. "Is this about what happened in the past?"

Travers smiled thoughtfully at her. "It always is."

A whole herd of butterflies took flight in her stomach. Dear God, what had she done? It could have been anything. Even the smallest ripple in time could potentially change the course of history. What if she'd eaten a piece of pie at the automat that someone really important was supposed to eat, like FDR, and he was so angry they didn't get his blueberry pie he never ran for president and we lost World War II?

"I'm sorry," she said.

Travers stopped rummaging in his briefcase and looked up in confusion. "For what?"

"For whatever I did." He squinted and shook his head. "I don't follow you."

Elizabeth paced across the room, but could only take two steps in the small apartment. Why wasn't her place big enough for a good solid pace? "I changed time, right? That's why you're here. It was an accident, you know. We didn't mean to activate the watch."

"We know," Peter said sympathetically. "And just to ease your mind, I'm not here because you changed time. Off the record, everything you did was just as it was meant to be."

Elizabeth stopped fidgeting and tried to get her mind around that. "I'm not sure I understand."

"Time is immutable. Or at least it's supposed to be," he added with a frown. "We're not really sure on that one."

Elizabeth stopped her mini-pace and considered the implications of that little admission.

"You were meant to go back to 1929," Travers continued. "Everything that happened there was meant to be. You working for Charlie Blue, meeting King, Sebastian Cross's…" His voice trailed off and cleared his throat.

"You know about all that?" She didn't know whether to be frightened or relieved or maybe just throw up a little.

"I studied your case file extensively before I destroyed it."

Definitely, leaning toward frightened. "I have a case file? Wait a minute. Destroyed it?"

"It was necessary."

"That doesn't sound good."

"It isn't," he said and then took a folder out of his briefcase. "We need your help."

There was something about those four little words that provoked clarity of mind. "What do you mean?"

Travers tilted his head to the side as if trying to figure how to say what needed to be said. Apparently not liking the answer, he tugged anxiously on his ear. "We have a…situation."

Euphemisms were never good. They were just a red flag for the big ugly lurking beneath a patina of vagueness. The Council's *situation*. Her and Simon's *arrangement*.

"I should call Simon," she said abruptly and started for the phone.

Turning a lighter shade of pale, he stepped into her path. "W-why don't you hear me out first? Then you can call him and tell him everything. That way y-you have something to tell him."

That sounded logical enough, and truth be told, Simon probably wouldn't answer the phone right now even if he was home. No one brooded like Simon. It was art.

"All right," she said. "But I am going to tell him everything you tell me. We don't have any secrets," she said, trying not to choke on that particular chunk of irony.

"Of course."

He seemed inordinately relieved that she wasn't calling Simon, but that thought was pushed away by a much more troubling one. "How do I know you're who you say you are?"

"Ah!" he said and reached into his briefcase, revealing a velvet pouch. Pulling the drawstring, he let the contents fall into his hand. Elizabeth's breath hitched. It was an antique pocket watch

19

just like Simon's grandfather's with the same Mercator map etched into its gold case.

A rush of memories swept over her as he placed it in her hand. She ran her fingers over the etching, afraid to open it. She'd learned the hard way that time travel devices were not to be treated casually.

"Go ahead," he said, indicating that she should open it. "Nothing will happen."

She knew he was right, there was no eclipse to activate it, but she still felt a tingle of fear as she opened the clasp.

It had the same complex dials and rings as Simon's. He moved closer to admire it. "Beautiful, isn't it?"

And dangerous. Elizabeth handed it back to him, but he refused it. "It's yours."

She held it out to him. "You've made a mistake."

His brow knitted and if it could, it would probably have purled too. "You are Elizabeth West, aren't you?"

She couldn't help but laugh, but the seriousness of what she held in her hand brought her back. "I am, but—"

Taking out his crumpled handkerchief, he mopped the beads of sweat that had spontaneously popped out on his forehead. "I told them I wasn't the right person for this assignment," he muttered to himself, before stuffing the cloth back into his pocket. "This isn't a joking matter."

Elizabeth looked down at the watch and tightened her hand around it. "I know."

"That watch is one of twelve. Nine are currently assigned and in the field. The tenth is, I believe, in Mr. Cross' safety deposit box at the National Bank on First."

"How do—"

Travers held up a hand to stop her. "The Council knows where all the watches are at any time and in any time. But that's not important. What is important is what you do now."

He gestured toward the sofa. "May I?"

Elizabeth nodded and he sat down uncomfortably, setting his briefcase down on the coffee table. He sat up straight and moved toward the edge of the cushion and cleared his throat. "The Council is need of your help. We find ourselves in a difficult situation."

"I don't mean to be blunt, Mr. Travers, but I don't see how that's my problem."

"I'm afraid it might become your problem."

Elizabeth didn't like the sound of that.

"We have reason to believe that time has been altered, or will be. It's difficult to explain, but our Council of Twelve is now a Council of Eleven."

"Someone quit?"

"Someone ceased to be."

"I don't understand."

"Charles Graham was a long-standing member of the Council and a fine field operative. Today, any trace, every record of his existence is gone. After some research, we discovered that his great-grandfather was murdered and never had children. Graham's grandfather, father and subsequently Graham himself were never born."

"But how is that possible? You said time was immutable."

"I said we thought it was. Apparently, we were wrong."

Elizabeth didn't know what to say to that. Our entire theory of time and space? Forget that. "But if time has changed, how do you know that it has? You're part of the new timeline and this is giving me a serious headache."

"The memory of his existence is already fading. Proximity to the watch somehow lets us remember how it once was, but that effect will fade in time too."

"Simon's grandfather Sebastian told him that there was a temporal wash from the watch."

"Yes, yes exactly. And to make matters worse—"

"Let's not do that," Elizabeth said.

"This moment in history is important to the Council in other ways as well. We don't know many details about the founding of the Council itself. The files are disturbingly vague actually. But we do know that the watchmaker, identity unknown, created the watches in early 1907. It's possible, he has some connection to the changing of events."

"I still don't see what this has to do with me or Simon. I'm sorry for Mr. Graham, but—"

"Ripples. One change leads to other changes. We're afraid that Graham's murder has the potential to change the shape of the Council, even its very existence. Ask yourself: If there's no Council, what does Sebastian Cross do? How does his life change? How do the lives of his children and their children change? Do they even exist?"

Elizabeth felt a chill run through her body and rubbed the goose bumps that covered her forearms. "You don't know that will happen."

"We believe it will. And if we don't act soon, we'll forget everything that's changed and it'll be too late. You'll never meet Simon Cross because Simon Cross will never have been born. And you won't even know it."

CHAPTER THREE

TRAVERS LEFT A FEW hours and a few hundred questions later. It was totally insane, but Elizabeth couldn't get past one thing—if she didn't try, the Simon she knew and loved might never exist. The very thought gave her a chill. It was bad enough to be fighting, to be afraid of losing him. But the idea of never even knowing him took her breath away.

The whole thing was hard to wrap her mind around. Time travel paradoxes and the endless possible permutations gave her that same glassy-eyed feeling she'd had in Mr. Talbot's calculus class. Things sort of made sense when she just let them come to her, but if she tried to hold onto something specific it squirted away like a greased pig at the county fair. In the end it didn't matter. No matter how hard she rubbed her brain cells together, her gut told her what she had to do.

According to Travers, Victor Graham was murdered sometime late Easter Sunday 1906. In, of all places, San Francisco. Why couldn't he be from Sheboygan? Travel back in time, stop a murder, and survive one of the worst earthquakes in history. Somehow she knew that would be easy-peasy lemon-squeezy compared to convincing Simon to go.

When she and Simon had first returned from 1929, she was as relieved as he was, what with them both nearly dying and all. But memory paints impressionistic portraits of the past, enhancing some images and blurring others. To her, the crucible didn't seem nearly as important as the things it forged—friendship, courage and love. But it had been traumatic. For both of them. Not to mention Simon's trust of the Council could fit inside a flea's belly button. Even though his own life might depend on it, she knew he'd resist.

To make matters worse, the clock was officially ticking. They had only two days until the eclipse that would allow the watch to take them back in time. She literally didn't have a minute to waste.

She pulled her Beetle up to the curb in front of Simon's place. She ignored her poor car's death rattle as it shook and shimmied before giving one last cough and shutting down. Anxious, but afraid of what might come, she looked out of the window and at Simon's house. The gentle glow of a single light from the study window filtered out into the quiet night making the house look like a dragon sleeping with one eye open. She tucked the folder under her arm. Time for a little slaying.

Clutching the file tightly, she walked up the dark path to Simon's house. She stumbled on an uneven cobblestone and swore under her breath. Even his house wasn't going to make this easy.

The door to his study stood ajar, the light jutting out in a sharp angle against the dark, hardwood floors. Gently, she pushed it open further. "Simon?"

Sitting forward in an overstuffed reading chair, his elbows resting on his knees, Simon stared down intently at his clasped hands. "Where have you been?"

For a split second, she felt her buttons being pushed, but she flipped the override switch and forged ahead. "You will not believe who I just talked to."

"Aumond?" he said, not bothering to hide his contempt.

"No," she said with a sigh. "I'm sorry about not discussing that with you sooner, but it doesn't matter."

He raised his head to meet her eyes. "It matters to me."

"I know, but…" she said and paced across the room. Now, *this* was a room built with a good pace in mind. "Aumond is small potatoes; we're talking the entire potato famine here."

"If you think I'm going to let what happened earlier go so easily…"

Elizabeth stopped pacing and turned to face him. Of course not. He wouldn't be Simon if he did. Soothing hurt feelings would have to wait though. She was going to bust if she didn't tell him what happened. "The Council came to see me."

Simon's head snapped back as if he'd been struck. He stared at her for a long moment before speaking in a voice that sounded like stone grinding against stone. "They what?"

"They came to—"

Simon surged out of his chair and was across the room and gripping her arms before she could finish her sentence. "You're to have nothing to do with them," he said fiercely. "Do you understand me?"

Elizabeth blinked in shock, before gathering her wits and wriggling out of his grasp. "I understand that you might seriously need some Valium," she said and massaged her arms. "What is the matter with you?"

Simon seemed to snap back to himself and then faltered. "I'm…"

"Slightly out of control?" She knew another parry was the wrong move. She needed to try to calm him and not provoke him, but the words spilled out.

25

They seemed to help him regain his footing. He fixed her with a piercing glare that held her more strongly than his hands ever could. "Don't ever speak to them again, Elizabeth. You have to promise me you won't."

"You don't even know what they asked me."

He turned quickly away and strode across the room, raking a hand through his hair. "It doesn't matter."

Had he lost the plot completely? Wasn't he even the least bit curious? "It does matter," she said with forced patience, before taking a breath. "That's what I'm trying to tell you. It matters a lot."

He stopped and stared at the far wall. "They'll just have to make do without your help."

Something didn't add up. She didn't expect him to take it in stride, but something wasn't right. "How did you know they wanted my help?" She felt the pang of a belatedly realized betrayal. Elizabeth tightened her grip on the folder and her surging anger. "They came to see you first, didn't they?"

Slowly, he turned around. "Yes, two days ago."

His frank admission, so matter of fact, stunned her. "And you were going to share this when?"

"That's irrelevant."

Oh, that was rich. "Wasn't irrelevant at lunch."

His eyes darted away from hers. "That was different."

The air was suddenly thick and heavy and impossible to breathe. The word hypocrite danced on the end of her tongue, but she forced it back down. They'd deal with that later. He'd survive that, but the Council's news was something else entirely. "What if everything they've said is true? Did you even consider that? Simon, your life is in danger."

"Lies."

"Did you even listen to what he had to say?"

"We've no reason to trust them," he said as though that answered her question.

Elizabeth huffed in disbelief. "We? I must have missed the 'we' part. Did that come before or after you decided what was best for me?"

"My grandfather died on one of their... missions," he said, practically spitting out the word. "Don't think that a day passes in my life when I don't remember how close I came to losing you. All because of that bloody Council. I'll be damned if I'll let it happen again."

"And I don't want to lose you!" Elizabeth took a deep breath and tried to calm down. "Would you at least listen to what I have to say?"

Simon rolled his shoulders and stalked to his desk. He planted himself in the chair and waved his hand giving her the floor. Only Simon could be completely accommodating and utterly condescending at the same time.

Not exactly a receptive audience, but at least he wasn't shouting anymore. Elizabeth gave him the Reader's Digest version of everything that Travers had told her.

When she was finished, Simon leaned back in his chair. "And why don't they send one of their own men? Why you?"

"They want someone outside of the Council. There's no telling how things have changed, how they might have been corrupted."

"No telling," Simon echoed. "Might have. A story spun of what-ifs and maybes."

He leaned forward, intense. "They're manipulating you."

That thought had crossed Elizabeth's mind. She really had no reason to trust the Council and several reasons not to. "Maybe they are."

Simon got out of his chair. "Finally, some sense."

Elizabeth smiled sadly. "But I'm not willing to risk the consequences if they're right."

"You're not doing this," Simon said.

The words were absolute, but she heard the doubt and fear inside them. "You can't control everything, Simon."

His hand sliced through the air. "It's not—Damn it." he said and let out a deep breath. "Elizabeth, if you love me—"

"I'm doing this *because* I love you, Simon. I had hoped that even if you didn't trust the Council, you'd trust me."

With that, she turned and walked out. If he had an answer he gave it to an empty room.

CHAPTER FOUR

His moment's hesitation at her departing declaration had cost him dearly. By the time he'd gathered himself enough to follow her she was already gone. Simon spent the next few hours searching for her without any luck. None of her friends had heard from her. He'd gone to her apartment, the office, even the damn library, and she was nowhere to be found. Clearly didn't want to be found.

He slammed the front door behind him as he returned home. "Damn!"

Simon's fantasies of finding her and talking some sense into her were just that, fantasies. He could have tied her to the bedposts and she would have found a way to go.

It was folly, pure unadulterated idiocy, and exactly the sort of thing she was wont to do. He'd known it from the moment she'd mentioned the Council. And like a fool, he'd challenged her. Even if she wasn't intent on going before, she surely was now.

The grandfather clock in the hall chimed ominously, each resounding clang marking the time he'd wasted. A litany of invectives streamed behind him like a comet's tail as he walked into his study.

Why was she so reckless? So trusting? What could she be thinking? She'd run off and get herself killed. For what? Because the Council said they needed her help? It was idiocy. It was naïve. It was… He drew up short. It was love.

She was doing this insane thing out of love. When it came to that, there was no stopping her. He'd been a fool. Again. He should have stood with her. He'd been so afraid of losing her, he'd completely ignored the fact that she felt the same way. The last time he let his fear get the better of him he pushed her away and nearly lost her. And now, he'd done it again.

The weight of that revelation pushed him down into a chair. He leaned forward and clasped his hands.

He should have trusted her, but his overriding need to protect her had trumped his common sense. Not that she wanted his protection or needed it, but he felt compelled to give it nonetheless. Despite what she thought, it wasn't because he saw her as incapable and it certainly had nothing to do with her being a woman. It did, however, have everything to do with her being the woman he loved.

There was a life's breath in being with her that he couldn't live without. But if he kept pushing her away, if he kept standing in front of her instead of beside her, he would lose her.

She was willing to risk everything for him and he'd dismissed her feelings completely. He really was a selfish bastard and damn her she was going to save him whether he deserved it or not.

He stood and strode over to his desk. Perhaps it was time to start deserving it, he thought. The fragmented feeling of helplessness was abruptly replaced by the firm conviction of singleness of purpose. He wasn't going to waste the next two days in a fruitless search. If she didn't want to be found, and it was clear she didn't, he wouldn't be able to find her. But that wouldn't stop him.

He'd be damned if he'd let her go alone. This time, though, he'd be prepared.

He turned on his blasted computer and pulled out his phonebook.

He remembered scant details from that blithering idiot Travers' tale to Elizabeth, but it was enough. It had to be enough. He remembered the date and location—April 9, 1906, San Francisco, just a little over one week before the catastrophic earthquake. That gave him pause. The San Francisco earthquake was nothing to be trifled with. If he remembered his history correctly, the quake was over 8.0 on the Richter scale and the fires that followed were even more devastating. He'd have to convince her to leave the city before then. A time and a place—not much to go on—but all he needed. Whatever Elizabeth was getting herself into, she wouldn't be in it alone and that was all that mattered.

He sat down in his desk chair and got to work.

Over the years he'd cultivated an extensive network of antiquity collectors and spent the next few hours waking, bullying and bribing them. The full complement of supplies had cost him an unconscionable sum, but he would have spent ten times that if needed. Money had never meant much to him, until he'd been forced to live without it. Traveling back in time to New York and living as a pauper had been an object lesson he wasn't soon to forget.

Antique national bank notes, the only reasonable currency of the time, with a face value of nearly ten thousand dollars were being sent by overnight courier. Explicit instructions had been given to his tailor. A suit appropriate for a wealthy man at the turn of the century with all accompanying accouterments would be ready by noon. No excess was too excessive. No expense too expensive. No possibility considered impossible. He'd even contacted the family solicitor and asked him to send a few important papers.

This time, he would arrive as a man of means. And those means had only one end—to do anything and everything to bring Elizabeth back safely.

By morning, Simon had completed all his preparations, save one. He was at the bank when it opened and accompanied the clerk to his safety deposit box. The teller placed the slender metal container on the table and left him to his privacy. The cyclone of manic planning dwindled until only an ill wind remained. When he'd put the watch away four months ago, he'd hoped it would be the last time he'd ever see it. Only an unbreakable allegiance to his grandfather had kept him from destroying it.

Slowly, he opened the lid to his own Pandora's box and a plague of personal demons was released. Picking up the watch, he held his only hope in his hand. The last time he'd held it, the watch had wielded him, controlled his fate. This time, he would wield it.

Simon tied the ivory cravat around his starched, white collar and looked at himself in the mirror. A gentleman of repute stared back. The tailor had outdone himself. Calfskin button boots settled just beneath the cheviot, dark grey twill of his trousers. A pristine, white shirt with stiff cuffs accented with sterling silver links stood out brightly against the pearl silk waistcoat and gloves.

Through his cutaway coat the money belt bulged above his hip, but there was nothing to be done for it. He'd been forced to acquire smaller denominations than he'd wanted and the result was an unseemly lump. Luckily, the weather in San Francisco hadn't changed in the last hundred years and his Chesterfield overcoat would still be de rigueur for early spring.

Money wasn't his only weapon, he thought as he slipped a 1905 Colt vest pocket pistol into his pocket. It was a small caliber gun, but the little magazine held six bullets. If he needed more than that, no gun, he feared, was going to be enough.

With only minutes to spare, he shrugged on his overcoat and pulled the felt-banded brim of his hat down. A spider's crawl of anticipatory dread inched up his spine, but he willed it away. Elizabeth needed him, whether she knew it or not, and he wasn't about to let her face whatever dangers awaited her alone. Armed with certitude of purpose, he opened the watchcase, stared down at the moon inset and waited.

He didn't have to wait long. The paralyzing, blue light sparked out of the watch and up his arm. The world around him shivered and he was plunged into darkness.

MONIQUE MARTIN

CHAPTER FIVE

Elizabeth struggled against the strange disconnected feeling until she felt her head definitely connect with something. Something… leafy? Managing to right herself, she stared at the offending bush before remembering to check for any witnesses. Thankfully, she was alone. Very, very alone. Damn you, Simon.

She'd spent the last day and a half trying to soak up the reams of information Travers had given her and trying not to think about what she was leaving behind. Besides, if everything went well, it would be like she'd never left. Except for the arguing and gargantuan emotional chasm they'd have to cross. She'd leap the Great Divide when she came to it. Right now she had a job to do, a Simon to save and twigs to get out of her hair. So much for the two hours she'd spent wrangling it into her best Gibson Girl imitation.

Victor Graham was a wealthy businessman and that meant he traveled in elite circles. Travers had meticulously given her a crash course in Victorian and Edwardian society. Just the word society had been enough to make her pulse race. Living with Simon had given her a glimpse at how the better half lived, but they weren't exactly on the social circuit. The closest she'd ever gotten to consorting with the horsey set was getting tips from the touts at the track. She was part of the great unwashed and had the dirt on her cheek to prove it. Thank God, Travers had insisted she stuff that kerchief into her sleeve. She glanced quickly around and spit into it before wiping her cheek.

A smooth start. Taking a header into a hedge and spitting. Her head pounded and her stomach was a little wiggly, but it was a heck of a lot better than the headbanger's ball she'd suffered through last time. Taking a deep breath she felt her ribs squish her innards.

The corset she could have done without. Torquemada had nothing on whatever sadist invented it. Compressing her breasts into some sort of one-eyed, monobosom monster, squeezing the life out of her stomach and thrusting her hips backward, it successfully contorted her body into what society of the early twentieth century deemed an acceptable shape. It was all she could do not to rip the dang laces and start the bra-burning age a few decades early.

Not being able to breathe was the least of her worries. She'd managed to arrive without passing out. Point one for her, although, she hadn't managed to move from that spot. Quickly, she took stock of her surroundings. Large oak trees canopied expansive, outlandishly colorful flowerbeds. Flaming oranges and deep reds swirled in complicated patterns amongst a vibrant purple like some tapestry gone mad. Enclosing the entire thing was a large, boxwood hedge, with whom she was already well acquainted.

This looked like the right place. Travers had said that if everything went well she'd arrive in the garden of Mrs. Eldridge's safe house. It was secluded from the street, thanks to her friend the hedge, and she could appear without scaring the living bejesus out of anyone. Herself notwithstanding.

Satisfied she was in one piece, and having stalled longer than was necessary, Elizabeth took a well-measured breath and headed for the front path. All she had to do was utter the simple code phrase Travers had given her and Mrs. Eldridge would give her whatever else she needed.

As she edged up the walkway, the mansion loomed even larger. Gothic and imposing. Steeply pitched gables and sharp arched windows made it look more like a cathedral than a home. The fleeting image of being held prisoner inside one of the pinnacle towers flashed in her mind. But she was no Rapunzel and her knight currently had his head up his ass. Just as she was having serious second thoughts, the front door opened and a young man and an elderly woman stepped out onto the porch.

"I'll be sure to give Mother your regards." The young man bounded down the stairs and nearly crashed into Elizabeth. "I beg your pardon," he said quickly taking off his goggles and cap. "Are you all right?"

"I'm...I'm fine," Elizabeth managed. "Thank you."

He smiled disarmingly. "The thanks is all mine," he said and then turned back to the elderly woman. "Where have you been keeping her?"

The woman, who simply had to be Mrs. Eldridge, lifted her pince-nez and arched an eyebrow. "In the garden, it appears."

The young man turned back to her and laughed. "You have," he said and waved a hand in the general direction of her hair, "an intruder."

Elizabeth patted at her hair.

"If you'd allow me?" he asked, and before she could protest, plucked a leaf from her hair.

"That was embarrassing," Elizabeth mumbled.

He turned on that smile of his again. "I think it was rather becoming. And I'll cherish it always," he said as he stuffed the leaf into his breast pocket. "Maxwell Alexander Harrington the Third, your humble servant," he added with a bow.

The older woman sighed and lowered her glasses. "You are incorrigible."

"You'll have to forgive me," he said, not taking his eyes off Elizabeth. "Love does strange things to a man."

"Ignore him," the woman said. "Riding in that new motorcar of his has scrambled his brain."

For a long moment, he didn't react, just simply stared at Elizabeth. It should have been discomfiting, but he exuded an earnestness no amount of brashness could cover. Handsome by any standards, he was the very definition of the All-American Boy—tall, easily over six feet, sun-streaked hair and a dimple in his chin you could crawl inside.

"And your manners," the older woman prompted. "How you could possibly be a relation of mine is beyond me."

"She's my distant aunt," he said by way of explanation.

"And growing more distant with every passing moment."

Elizabeth liked her immediately. She was Helen Hayes with attitude. "I didn't mean to interrupt."

She waved her hand dismissively. "No, no. Maxwell was just leaving. What can I do for you, dear?"

Elizabeth's throat went dry. This was the moment of truth. "Mr. Holland sent me."

A brief flicker of surprise and then recognition crossed the woman's face before she smiled as though Elizabeth had just complimented her prized petunias. "Oh, isn't that lovely," she said coming down a few steps and holding out her hand. "I haven't heard from him in ages. Won't you come inside dear and you can tell me how everyone's doing?"

Just like that Elizabeth was being shuttled into the house.

"Another of your secret liaisons, Aunt Lillian?" Max said, trailing behind.

Mrs. Eldridge never stopped escorting Elizabeth inside and merely said over her shoulder, "Goodbye, Maxwell," and promptly shut the door behind them. Once they were a few feet into the entry hall she squeezed Elizabeth's arm gently. "Welcome to 1906, dear."

Simon's dizzying journey from intangible to tangible ended abruptly, punctuated with a hard fist connecting flush with his chin.

The vague light of consciousness dimmed as he stumbled backwards and collided with something. The painful grunt in his ear told him that something was a man. Loud, garbled voices he couldn't understand reverberated around him causing the sharp pain in his jaw to radiate up to join the timpani in his temple.

Simon took a tentative step forward and shook his head trying to clear it. His vision was still blurry, but he had enough faculties left to know that one blow was usually followed by another. He tried to steady himself for the next attack and realized there wasn't one man standing in front of him; there were six. All of them wore identical, over-sized, dark blue silk sacks and trousers and shocked expressions. Braided queues of black hair peeked out from beneath their flat-brimmed hats.

Tendrils of sandalwood smoke wafted between them and Simon's eyes followed them back to the source. Lines of Joss-sticks billowed with incense. Bright red banners fluttered in the breeze down the narrow cobblestone street.

"Gangui!" one of the men cried. *"Gangui!"*

As his muddled brain instinctively recognized the phrase, the last piece of the puzzle slipped into place. Dear God, Simon thought. I've landed in China.

CHAPTER SIX

"GANGUI!"

The men who surrounded Simon were confused and frightened. Judging from their expressions and what he knew of Chinese mythology, they seemed to think he was some sort of demon. Simon rifled through his mind searching for some way to press his advantage. Surely, it wouldn't last long.

Even before that discouraging thought had taken root the leader stepped forward and quieted his men with a harshly barked order. Once sure they feared him more than any demon, the leader turned and gave Simon an exceedingly discomfiting appraisal. The vague shadow of fear lingered in his eyes, but keen logic was winning out. The initial shock of Simon's arrival was wearing off and the incongruity of a Chinese demon appearing as a white man, all irony aside, begged questions Simon didn't want asked. The man lifted his chin in defiance and spoke to Simon in what was clearly a challenge.

When Simon didn't reply, the shadow of fear disappeared completely from the man's eyes, replaced with the spark of advantage gained. Simon's heart beat faster. The odds of survival were getting worse with every passing second. The leader asked the question again and then turned to address his men. Whatever he said rallied them and they laughed, nervously at first, but with growing confidence.

As the leader turned back, Simon did the only thing he could. He pulled the pistol out of his pocket and took aim squarely at the man's head. The laughter died. After a brief flash of surprise, the leader narrowed his eyes in a quick study of his opponent. His gaze flicked over the pistol and Simon could almost see him calculating the odds of triumph or defeat. Six bullets. Six men.

Simon held the pebbled grip in his hand already feeling the sweat forming in his palm. His arm was steady enough, although from this distance they could rush him before he got off more than two shots. Forcing his mind to clear as best he could, Simon met the leader's gaze. In a silent trial of wills they stared at each other. Simon felt the other men's eyes boring into him, but he didn't dare look away.

The leader held Simon's gaze with smooth confidence, content to wait for him to falter first. But Simon held fast and the tension grew between them. Adrenaline coursed through Simon's veins. When the man's mouth creased into a small smile, Simon gripped the gun more tightly. His finger gently took up the slack in the trigger.

The penultimate moment dangled on the precipice until finally the leader broke eye contact. Prepared for a veiled signal to the men, Simon held the gun steady.

As if Simon weren't even there, the leader turned his attention to someone behind him. Simon dared a quick glance back and saw an injured man just rousing to consciousness. The leader spoke to the man in Chinese, and while the words were foreign the intent was a promise that whatever Simon had interrupted wasn't over. With one last look to Simon and a brief nod ceding this round, the leader ordered his men to leave.

Simon kept his gun trained on them as they filtered into the crowd and disappeared down the street. It was only after he was sure they'd gone he let out the breath he'd been holding. One crisis down and who knew how many to go. His palm was slick with sweat and he wiped it on his trouser leg and then slipped the gun back into his pocket. The crowd continued to stream down the street seemingly oblivious to the drama. Each person kept to their own business, averting their eyes and hurrying on their way.

It was just as well. The sooner he got off this street the sooner he could get the hell out of China. Damn watch. Like a fool, he looked down at his hand—one gun and no watch. The realization was like cold water thrown in his face.

It has been knocked out of his hand when he'd been struck. Desperately, he scanned the street gathering his hat along the way, and found the watch nestled between two crates of squawking, pungent chickens. He picked it up and prayed it hadn't been damaged. Aside from a fresh scratch along the case, it appeared to be intact. Of course, he couldn't be certain until he used it again, and God only knew when the next eclipse was.

His jaw ached and his head was still swimming.

Forcing his hat into some semblance of its previous shape, he started down the street when he heard the injured man groan. Simon stopped, but didn't turn. It wasn't any of his affair. He had his own problems to deal with. As he took a step away, a niggling voice in his head stopped him. The niggling voice that sounded remarkably like Elizabeth's had become the point to his counterpoint. Even in the confines of his own mind, he was no match for her. It seemed that despite his best efforts her damnable altruistic nature had infected him. Heaving a defeated sigh he turned back to the man.

It was the first time he'd given him a good look and Simon realized how truly incongruous he was. He was undoubtedly Chinese, but his clothes were Western. He was probably in his early thirties. His black, three-button suit wasn't well-tailored, but still a good quality and definitely Western. Blood trickled from his split lip and stained the white of his collar.

"Can you stand?" Simon said as he held out his hand. The man looked at him in confusion. "Stand?" Simon repeated in the time-honored tradition of English speakers everywhere that any words enunciated clearly and loudly enough would be understood.

The man eyed him warily but accepted Simon's help and managed to get to his feet. He stood for a moment on unsteady legs then stumbled forward and gripped the wall for balance. Simon reached out to steady him.

The man gestured that he could stand on his own and stared intently at Simon. His voice was quiet, but words hit Simon like a cartoon anvil. "Thank you."

Simon's hand tightened around the man's arm. "You...you speak English?"

"Is it so surprising?" he said, reaching into his pocket for a white handkerchief and dabbing at the blood on his chin.

"Bloody hell. Of course it is."

"Not every Chinese immigrant is content to be a Coolie," he said in perfect English as he refolded his handkerchief and pushed it back into his pocket. He seemed to mistake Simon's stunned expression for disapproval and quickly amended, "And that was ungracious. Forgive me."

Simon ignored the insult and the apology. "Immigrant? Where are we?"

The man arched an eyebrow. "San Francisco." He looked Simon up and down. "Perhaps I should be the one helping you?"

"Chinatown," Simon said. Any embarrassment he felt over his misconception was lost in the realization that Elizabeth couldn't be far away. "Thank God. Which direction is downtown?"

"This way," the man said as he stepped out into the street.

Simon hesitated. He had no reason to trust him, and, Elizabeth's voice whispered in his mind, no reason not to.

"We should leave this place. Ling Tan and his men will be back soon and I'm afraid they won't be unarmed this time. Unless you have a Gatling gun hidden in your trousers, I suggest we leave here as soon as possible. The tong is not forgiving."

Simon didn't know much about San Francisco history, but he knew enough about Chinese gangs to know they needed to leave. Now. "Agreed."

They made their way up the narrow alley until they emerged onto a larger thoroughfare. The cramped confines of Chinatown gave way to the broad elegance of the city.

A cable car bumped its way up the street, the wheels grinding out a shrill symphony on the metal tracks. It paused and people clambered onto the crowded fringe.

"This is our car," the man said, climbing on board.

Simon stepped onto the small platform and reached for his money, but the man had already paid their fare. "It's the least I can do."

Simon nodded his thanks and didn't argue the point.

"More sherry, dear?" Mrs. Eldridge asked Elizabeth as she took the crystal top from the decanter on the coffee table.

Elizabeth shook her head declining politely and shifted uncomfortably on the settee. Even though Mrs. Eldridge had done everything she could to make her feel at home, as Elizabeth looked around the salon, she felt anything but that.

The room was tastefully posh, although, between the wallpaper, the wainscoting, the rugs and the upholstery there were enough patterns to make her feel slightly nauseous. Other than that, it was the very image of elegant wealth. A little gilt here, a little velvet there, a little bit of lots of money everywhere.

"You're sure?" Mrs. Eldridge asked holding up the decanter. A large bay window let in the last rays of the setting sun and they danced in the facets of the crystal.

"No, thank you." Aside from the fact that her corset had gone all anaconda on her once she'd sat down, the sherry was making her head spin. No wonder women swooned so much. They couldn't get any blood to their heads.

"My husband always found it to be rather restorative after his travels."

"Your husband was a—he traveled too?"

Mrs. Eldridge set down the decanter and smiled wistfully. "For nearly forty years."

"Wow."

Mrs. Eldridge laughed softly and settled herself back into the plush divan. "You are new to this aren't you?"

"Does it show that much?"

"Only around the edges. Don't worry, dear. You'll do fine."

Elizabeth took a sip of sherry and suddenly wished it were something stronger. "I suppose you get used to it after a while."

"No. Never that. And if it does, you've gone one too many times. But I don't think you have to worry about that for some time. You've got enough on your plate as is. Another tea cake?" she added with a grin.

"Thank you, no. I…are you…?"

The older woman shook her head. "'They also serve, those who stand and wait.' Sometimes I think being the one left behind is the more difficult task."

Elizabeth felt a fresh wave of guilt wash over her. Simon. She'd been so angry, so caught up in trying not to think about how mad she was at him, she'd nearly forgotten how much she missed him. Not that it wasn't his own damn fault, but still.

"I don't understand," Elizabeth said. "If things work the same here as they do for me…"

"Waiting comes in many ways, dear. I used to think waiting for him to leave was the worst part."

The rest was left unsaid, but Elizabeth knew what the worst part must have been. The day he didn't return. "I'm sorry."

Mrs. Eldridge sighed and glanced at the portrait over the mantle in the parlor. The man in the portrait was a nice looking man in his sixties with silver hair and a kindly face. Mrs. Eldridge seemed lost in the murky haze of memories for a moment before smiling and regaining herself. "Another tenet of time travel—always live in the present, wherever and whenever that may be. And your present looks to be quite interesting."

Interesting was one way to put, Elizabeth thought as she nibbled on a biscuit. She wondered if Mr. Eldridge could be affected if she failed. He was part of the Council. Wait. Something didn't make sense. How could Mrs. Eldridge's husband have been a Council member if the Council hadn't even been created in 1906. Unless…

"When was Mr. Eldridge from?"

"1982, I think. We met in Chicago. He was on an assignment." Her smile was wistful. "And decided to stay. Of course, he did go back on occasion. Temporal commuting, he called it. He continued to work for the Council, but he always came home to me."

"I'm surprised the Council was okay with that."

"Evan could be quite persuasive." Mrs. Eldridge smiled kindly and continued. "Now, how can I help you?"

"You have anything stronger than sherry?"

Mrs. Eldridge laughed. "Perhaps later. I'm sure Gerald has something hidden away."

"I'm not sure where to start. I missed the time travel extension course."

"Well, typically, Council members don't discuss any details of their assignments, but in your case, perhaps we could bend that rule just a tad. Extenuating circumstances and all."

"Oh, they're extenuating all over the place."

"Why don't you start at the beginning, dear?"

CHAPTER SEVEN

THE SMALL PUDDLES OF light cast by the street lamps glowed on the sidewalk in front of them, illusive beacons of warmth in the growing chill. Simon wrapped his overcoat more tightly about him and tried not to think about Elizabeth.

He'd been so caught in the minutiae of each moment, planning his arrival and surviving same, he'd barely considered the breadth of the task at hand. With each block they walked, it seemed as big as the city itself. Not to mention given what he'd already experienced, there was no telling what she faced. He could only hope Travers had done his job well and God help him if he hadn't.

"Here we are," the Chinese man said, pulling him back to the matter at hand.

Simon stopped walking and surveyed the street. Black horse drawn carriages hurried past. While the buildings had grown larger and the stench of chickens seemed left far behind, he still had no idea where he was. "And where might that be?"

"Downtown. I believe you said that was your destination."

"Right," Simon said and peered down the dark streets. "Thank you."

Each building looked much the same as the next. He could wander aimlessly for hours trying to find a suitable place to stay. Then he remembered that he'd stayed at the Palace Hotel on his last trip to San Francisco. That time, he'd come hoping to purchase a rare Aubin Codex, but like so many other trips he'd left frustrated and empty handed. This would not be one of those times.

"The Palace Hotel?"

The man nodded and after a few long blocks, he motioned toward a broad archway leading to the entrance of a large upscale hotel.

If the lobby was anything to judge by, the Palace Hotel was truly turn of the century opulence at its best. Heavy mahogany tables, red leather chairs, and ten-foot palms filled the spacious floor that easily spanned fifty by one hundred feet. It was a welcome taste of civilization.

"Is there anything else I can do?"

Simon mentally ran through the details he knew of Elizabeth's assignment. They were pathetically scant. He couldn't even remember the name of the man who was supposedly killed. At the time, he hadn't thought any of it mattered. Idiot.

"No," Simon said, extending his hand. "Thank you."

The man shook his head and bowed. "Thank *you*." With that he left Simon alone in the hotel.

The lobby was a hub of activity. Dozens of people milled about; some coming, some going, none of them knowing the devastation that was to come. And out there, somewhere, was Elizabeth. His Elizabeth.

He walked up to the front desk. He'd made it this far. That was something, at least. Now, all he had to do was find her. One woman in a city of half a million.

She was beautiful.

As he removed the pins from her hair, each tendril that fell and caressed her bare shoulder was a prelude to his touch. He'd planned to travel slowly, but the sloping curve of the nape of her neck was too much of a temptation. As he placed a gentle kiss on her shoulder, her sharp intake of breath broke the last vestiges of his restraint. He tightened his hands around her arms and he turned her to face him. Wrapping his arms around her, he pulled her half-dressed body flush against his. Lost in the midst of passion, he whispered her name. "Elizabeth."

The sound of his own voice woke him from the dream.

Simon opened his eyes and in an instant the warmth in his chest cooled. Long before he summoned the courage to turn his head, he knew she wouldn't be there. Even knowing the truth, he couldn't stop himself from looking.

Closing his eyes he fought the discontinuity, trying to find some foothold on a dream lost in the morning sun. Nightmares had haunted him for years, but in the end, dreams were proving to be far crueler.

Ignoring the unease he felt at the unfamiliar room, Simon tossed the sheet aside. Dreams and nightmares might taunt him at night, but in the day, reality was his to shape.

Simon headed for the bathroom and prayed there was a shower. He would settle for a bath if need be, but they always reminded him of being a child. Very few of his childhood memories were pleasant.

He opened the heavy paneled door from his bedroom suite and turned up the flame on the gas lamp. The concierge had assured him that the Palace had every amenity and he hadn't exaggerated. The bath was as well-appointed as the rest of his suite, although, he could do without the bidet. Leave it to the French.

Dark mahogany-paneled wainscoting covered the walls from trellised light wood ceiling to the mosaic tile floor. A brass framework of pipes that looked more like some medieval torture device than a shower wrapped itself around the inside of the standing shower enclosure. His grandfather's estate in Sussex had a similar contraption and as a boy he used to pretend it was the exposed ribcage of a vanquished giant. Of course, that was when monsters had no life outside of books and stories, when turning the page had kept him safe.

How time changes things, Simon thought as he carefully turned on the taps. Cool water sprang out in thin arching streams from a series of holes in each of the pipes. After some adjustment, the temperature was tolerable and he stepped inside.

After his shower, Simon wrapped a large bath towel about his waist. At least now, he felt marginally prepared to meet the day. He wiped the steam off the mirror and ran a hand over his stubbled chin. Hardly an appropriate look for entering society, but he hadn't brought his shaving kit, or a change of underwear for that matter. His mood soured distinctly.

Rubbing a towel over his damp hair, Simon walked back into his bedroom. Glaring down at his day olds, he heard a muffled knock coming from the front door. Hoping it was the tea he'd arranged for the night before, he headed for the main parlor.

The bedroom suite gave way to a long hall connecting to the parlor. Knuckles rapped smartly on the front door again. Simon draped the towel around his neck, quickly put on the hotel's complimentary dressing gown and yanked open the door.

A young steward swallowed so hard his Adam's apple nearly jumped out of his throat.

Simon waited, but nothing but a squeak emerged from the young man. "My tea?"

"I'm sorry sir. I'll see about the tea, but the tailor you requested is here."

The young man nervously stepped aside and an obsequious little man popped into view. Adjusting the tape measurer draped around his neck and pushing his black spectacles back onto the bridge of his nose, he smiled too broadly. "Anton Brandise, at your service Sir Simon," he said with a bow, as his eyes took in Simon in an appreciative sweep.

Simon gripped the edges of the towel around his neck and glared at the little man. When their eyes met, a blush stole over Mr. Brandise's face and he quickly averted his eyes.

Mr. Brandise cleared his throat then clapped his hands. "My trunk, boy."

The steward wheeled a large trunk to the door, but Simon blocked his path. "Sir?"

For a moment, Simon considered turning them away, but the unpleasant prospect of having his inseam measured by Mr. Brandise was ultimately outweighed by necessity. Simon stepped out of the way and the steward wheeled the heavy trunk into the room, setting it down with a thud.

"Be careful with that, boy!" Mr. Brandise barked then turned to Simon, his eyes drifting over Simon's chest again. "So hard to find good help these days, isn't it?"

Simon stared down at the tailor in disapproval and a not so subtle reminder of who was working for whom. "Isn't it?"

The steward beat a hasty retreat and closed the door behind him.

Mr. Brandise opened his trunk to reveal a full compliment of clothing and accessories. "I'm sure you'll find Brandise and Merchant has the best gentlemen's wares in the city. Perhaps something in the way of hounds-tooth?"

"I'll need four pairs of trousers to start," Simon said, not wanting this to take any more time than was absolutely necessary. "Striped worsted or cashmere. Black, dark brown or steel grey. Matching cutaway coats suitable for morning, business and day. Pinstripes no larger than an eighth of an inch. One suit, preferably black, for informal evening wear. And a complete formal arrangement including top hat. With all necessary accessories—waistcoats, cravats, collars, cuffs. And no hounds-tooth. Do you think you can manage that, Mr. Brandise?"

The tailor took out his kerchief and wiped his brow. "Yes, of course. It will take some time though."

"Time is something I don't have Mr. Brandise. If you can accommodate me by this time tomorrow you'll be well recompensed. If not, our business is finished."

Stuffing his kerchief back into his pocket he bowed his head. "I'm sure we can accommodate your needs."

"Very good. Now unless you plan on measuring me from there I suggest you produce suitable undergarments for me to wear as soon as possible."

The big blob of strawberry jam landed smack dab on Enrico Caruso. No wonder Simon had always insisted on spreading the jam for her when they had breakfast in bed. She was a stain waiting to happen. Thankfully, this morning's disaster had been narrowly averted thanks to Mr. Caruso and the newspaper. His scheduled appearance at the Grand Opera House was the most anticipated event of the season. It would bring the house down all right. His debut performance was the night before the earthquake. Elizabeth tried to put that thought out of her head and quickly wiped the smear off Enrico. Luckily, Mrs. Eldridge didn't notice.

Breakfast was an elegant affair: Silver service trays, delicate china and plenty of wonderful food. Elizabeth had tried to eat, but her corset had other ideas. She'd barely managed to force some toast and tea down when she started to feel uncomfortably full. Maybe she could market the corset diet on QVC when she got back home. First though, she had to save the world, or at least her part of it.

"Don't like my eggs?"

Elizabeth jumped at the voice. Gerald, Mrs. Eldridge's butler, was standing behind her. His natural expression was just this side of surly.

He was definitely not what Elizabeth had been expecting. She'd always envisioned butlers and valets as Jeevesy, expressionless automatons. Gerald was anything but that.

She guessed he was in his mid-fifties. It was hard to tell. His face was craggy with more than age. Despite his age and a slight limp, he was a powerful, raw sort of presence. His brick red hair grew off his head in angry waves. Bits of gray around the temples softened the overall effect, but with broad shoulders and at just over six feet tall, he cut an imposing figure.

His relationship with Mrs. Eldridge was another surprise. She was the boss, there was no doubt about that; she was everyone's boss. But their relationship was more than that. There was an ease with each other and a mutual admiration that she was sure wasn't typical for mistress and servant.

Gerald nodded his head toward her plate.

"Oh, no, I'm sorry. I was just—" Elizabeth said and quickly shoveled a forkful of cold scrambled eggs into her mouth. Gerald watched her without expression. Elizabeth smiled gamely as she forced down the rubbery bits. "Good."

Gerald's hard face cracked into a smile and he laughed. It was a deep, scratchy rumble and Elizabeth liked him immediately for it.

"Gerald," Mrs. Eldridge chided.

"Just testing, Lillian," he said. "Nice to a fault, this one."

"Is cook ill again?" Mrs. Eldridge asked.

Gerald picked up Elizabeth's plate and gave her a quick wink. "Probably ate some of her own cooking."

"Or yours," Mrs. Eldridge said going back to the paperwork she'd been doing.

"Cook should be back this afternoon."

Mrs. Eldridge peered up from her papers, looking over her glasses. She smiled slyly. "Thank you, Gerald."

Gerald gave her a small bow and left.

"He's a wonderful butler and a dear friend, but a horrible cook," she confided after he'd left. She took off her glasses and studied Elizabeth intently. "Now, as to your search for Mr. Graham. I think I might be able to help you on that count."

"It could be dangerous. I don't want you involved any more than you already are."

"Aren't you a dear? A few introductions," Mrs. Eldridge said taking a sip of her tea. "What could be the harm in that?"

That sounded ominous, but before Elizabeth could ask what she meant, she heard loud voices out in the hall. The voices grew louder and the door opened with a flourish. Maxwell Alexander Harrington III swept in like Lawrence of Arabia, pulled off his driving goggles and dirty, cream colored topcoat and tossed them carelessly on a chair. "I'll buy you new petunias, Aunt Lillian."

Mrs. Eldridge, who didn't seem the least surprised by his abrupt entrance, calmly walked to the window and peered out. "They're begonias. And you certainly will."

Maxwell raised his hands in submission when he noticed Elizabeth. "Well, hello again. So you weren't a dream."

Mrs. Eldridge sighed heavily, but Max ignored her. "Aren't you going to introduce us? Really, Aunt Lillian. Where are your manners?"

"Elizabeth West, it's my dubious pleasure to introduce my nephew, Maxwell. I believe he nearly ran you over yesterday."

"An accident. A most fortuitous accident," he said as he took Elizabeth's hand.

He smelled like lavender and gasoline.

Mrs. Eldridge turned from the window. "And a developing theme."

Max, still holding Elizabeth's hand, took the seat next to her, one knee almost on the ground, the very picture of the earnest suitor. Maybe it was the lighting, but she could have sworn one of the honey colored flecks in his light brown eyes actually twinkled. It was all Elizabeth could do not to giggle.

"And what brings you to our fair city, Miss West? It is Miss, isn't it?" he asked, flashing blindingly white teeth set off by his deep tan.

None of which she should be noticing. Even if her heart was in tiny little pieces, they belonged to Simon. She pulled her hand out of his grasp and smiled her best "genteel, but watch your boundaries" smile.

"I'm sorry," he said, running his fingers through his floppy blond hair. "I'm a bit of a fool when it comes to a beautiful woman."

That remark won him a delicate snort from Mrs. Eldridge.

"Somehow I find that hard to believe," Elizabeth said.

Mrs. Eldridge returned to her seat at the table. "Maxwell is quite the man about town."

There was little doubt of that. He was ridiculously charming and painfully handsome, the sort who could jump over a tennis court net and somehow not look like a complete jackass.

"I wouldn't go that far, Aunt Lillian. More tea?" he asked Elizabeth, holding up the pot.

The thought of another cup made her stomach gurgle in a most un-genteel way. Her eyeballs were already floating. "No, thank you. Five's my limit."

He laughed and set down the pot. "Oh, I do like her, Aunt Lillian."

"Then make yourself useful," Mrs. Eldridge said. "Get that… thing out of my flower bed and clean yourself up."

"Yes, Aunt Lillian," he said with a sigh.

"You're taking Elizabeth out."

"Yes, Aunt Lillian," he said with much more enthusiasm.

Before Elizabeth could protest, Mrs. Eldridge continued. "Control yourself. She needs an introduction to Victor Graham. I believe you're acquaintances. Do you think you can manage that without crashing into something?"

"It would be my pleasure," he said with a broad smile.

Elizabeth wasn't sure this was the best idea. How was she ever going to get anything done with the Great Leslie glued to her side? Not that she really had much of a choice.

Elizabeth smiled as demurely as twenty years of independence would allow. "This is very kind of you, Mr. Harrington."

He grasped her hand and helped her stand. If they'd had them in 1906, his smile would have flipped the circuit breakers. "Call me Max."

CHAPTER EIGHT

"Simon. Simon Cross."

The man behind the desk gave the pages of his book a circumspect study. "I'm sorry, sir. I don't see you on the list."

The concierge at the Palace had recommended the Haven as the most prestigious private club for a man of means. Judging from the haughty indifference of the man behind the desk and the expensive smelling cigar smoke wafting under the large oak double doors, it was the perfect place to find the people he needed to meet. "I'm not surprised. I've just arrived in town."

"I see. And your references? Do you have a letter from a member?"

Simon had expected that and pulled an envelope from the inner breast pocket of his overcoat. He handed it to the clerk.

Inside was a tidy bribe and formal paper. The man smiled as he pocketed the money and handed the paper back to Simon.

"I'm sorry for the misunderstanding, Sir Simon."

Simon handed him a few more bills. "I'm sure you'll find that adequate for my initial dues."

"Forgive me, Sir Simon. I'm sure I've misplaced your letter of introduction."

He opened a small drawer in the desk and pulled out a piece of paper. "Here it is," he said as he wrote Simon's name onto an empty space on what was obviously a well-prepared letter for just such an occasion. "Ah yes. I see you're an acquaintance of Major Tuttle. The Major is rather forgetful. Hasn't been the same since that business with Spain, I'm afraid. Doesn't get out much anymore."

For once, Simon was pleased his low opinion of human nature had been proven correct. "Of course."

"Welcome to Haven, Sir Simon."

"Your chariot awaits," Max said as he opened the gate to the street with a flourish. "You aren't afraid of automobiles, are you? Don't believe anything my aunt says. I assure you it's an entirely safe form of transportation. The horseless carriage is the wave of the future."

Elizabeth swallowed her smile. "I'm sure."

She didn't know what she'd been expecting, but it definitely wasn't something so beautiful. His car, although still nestled in Mrs. Eldridge's flowerbed, was exquisite. And huge. It had to be nearly twenty feet long.

Catching her smile, Max quickly moved to rub dirt off one of the brass, gas lamp headlights. "She's something, isn't she? Had her sent over from England a few weeks ago."

"She's amazing." She'd never been one to pay much attention to cars, just enough to keep her Bug running, but this was a work of art. Everything about it was elegant and powerful. It was a sleek convertible with an aquiline hood and broad sloping fenders. The cream colored paint, she realized, matched his suit.

"The English don't do much well," Max said. "But Rolls knows what they're doing when it comes it automobiles."

"Rolls Royce?"

Max seemed inordinately pleased. "You've heard of them? The 40/50. Finest automobile I've seen. I'm a bit of an aficionado. Planning on making the Peking to Paris rally next year. That's off the cuff, mind you, nothing official yet."

Dear God, it was the Great Race. He really was the Great Leslie. "Sounds very exciting."

Max dug under one of the seats and produced another pair of goggles and a topcoat. "Driving with me is always exciting."

He gestured for her to come around to the left side, as the steering wheel was on the right, and helped her into what was obviously a coat meant for a woman. Max was nothing if not prepared for the ladies.

"Perfect fit."

He took her hand, helped her up onto the running board and into the seat which was more like a large leather reading chair for two than any car seat she'd ever known. After tucking in her voluminous skirts, she took the offered goggles. There was a windshield, but it was far too small to offer much protection. Great. It took her five minutes to get the dang hat on straight in the first place. The feathered plume tickled her nose as she took out the pins.

Max moved around to the driver's side and flipped a switch. Gently, he eased a few levers on the steering wheel into position then jumped out again.

"Have it going in a tick," he said as he moved to the front and inserted the crank. He fiddled with the choke for a moment and then gave the crank two robust turns. The engine roared to life and Elizabeth gripped her seat. The sound was nearly deafening and the entire car shimmied in place. Securing the crank, he jogged back to the car and moved a few more levers.

"Off we go," he said as he released the parking brake on the right-side running board and simultaneously manipulated two of the three pedals on the floor.

They lurched forward as the wheels finally got a grip in the beleaguered flowerbed and bumped off the curb. Without a seatbelt to be found, Elizabeth nearly bounced out of her seat. Where was Ralph Nader when you really needed him?

Across the street a horse pranced nervously in place in front of its carriage. The driver pulled the reins in with one hand and made a very unpleasant gesture with the other. Max waved back as they trundled down the street.

Even though they were only going about twenty miles an hour the world passed by in a blur. Between the bumpy ride and the deep scratch on her goggles, which no matter how you sliced it, did not bode well, she could barely see anything. Apparently, Max couldn't see much either as he narrowly swerved around another carriage. He squeezed the rubber bulb of the car's horn and a loud squawking honk came out. That and the sound of another angry carriage driver were left behind them as they sped away.

They were seriously picking up speed as he rolled down one of San Francisco's ubiquitous hills. Elizabeth glanced down to see if Max was riding the brake. That is if they had brakes. Just in case, she tightened her death grip on the seat's edge.

The street was crowded, but Max didn't seem to mind as he careened in and out among the slower moving carriages. The intersection ahead was congested with cross-traffic, but Max didn't seem to notice. Just as they were about to broadside a cable car, he gripped a lever on the running board and a high-pitched screech joined the roar of the engine. Dampening their speed barely enough, Max made the hard left turn.

The force of the turn caused her to slide across the small loveseat, flush against Max. "Handles like a gem, doesn't she?" he yelled in her ear over the engine noise.

It was reckless and totally out of control. And Elizabeth loved it. The anxiety that had balled up in her stomach started to loosen up. She gripped the seat and yelled over the din. "This as fast as she goes?"

Max grinned and pulled down his cap. Elizabeth held on for the ride of her life.

Oliver Wentforth droned on interminably. Normally, listening to a Civil War veteran would have fascinated Simon, but the man made even the Battle of Antietam boring.

Simon had been in the Haven for barely an hour and already he was reassessing his strategy, but he knew he was in the right place. As much as men denied it, they gossiped like old women in clubs like this. The main topic of conversation was, not surprisingly, women. If a beautiful woman had just arrived in town, he'd be sure to hear about it in a place like this. God help him.

Long ago he'd forsaken this very sort of life for the very sort of reasons he wanted to stuff Wentforth's Meerschaum pipe down his throat. Pompous and wildly embellished, his retellings of the historic battle made Simon want to cringe, but he dutifully played his part and nodded, adding the occasional requisite grunt of agreement.

Several puffs on Wentforth's pipe gave Simon the opening he was looking for. "Fascinating," he said as he shifted his seat and hopefully the conversation. "Tell me, Gardiner. Did you serve in the army too?"

Reginald Gardiner sniggered and Simon took that as a no. He'd doubted Gardiner was the military sort, but any change in conversation would be a welcome one. And Gardiner seemed much more the sort of man Simon wanted to be acquainted with. From his fastidiously trimmed mustache and the overwhelming smell of brilliantine, he was obviously someone who thought himself a ladies' man. Wedding ring, not withstanding. Foppish and lascivious was usually a combination Simon wouldn't tolerate, but in this case, it was exactly what he needed.

Gardiner played with the ends of his mustache as his laughter died down. "Good gracious, no. I'll leave that sort of thing to men like Wentforth. I prefer a more personal battle, if you get my meaning."

Wentforth scowled and puffed out his pipe smoke with distaste. "Reg, really."

Gardiner shrugged and gave Simon a surreptitious wink. "All men have vices. For some it's drink. Others laudanum," he added, causing Wentforth to puff erratically. "Man is a flawed creature. Woe to woman for she is stuck with the likes of us."

If this was the sort of man Elizabeth was forced to consort with, he couldn't find her soon enough. "Ah, but what a wonderful thing to be stuck to, no?"

"Oh, or stuck in," Gardiner said with a wink.

It was all Simon could do not to throttle the man. Somehow, he managed a weak smile.

"A kindred spirit. I think that calls for a drink," Gardiner said with a haphazard wave to a waiter. "Cross?"

"A bit early for me, but—"

"Oh, come now. It's never too early. I'll order you some eggs to go with it if it pleases you."

Simon forced out a short laugh. "No, thank you. But I might take you up on that drink later tonight."

Gardiner pouted like a small boy. "Oh, if only I could. Caroline is having another of her famous dinner parties. God help me. And you think he's boring," he added with a nod toward Wentforth.

Simon sensed his opening, but months of playing cards with Elizabeth had taught him never to play his hand too early. "Surely it isn't that bad?"

"You have no idea," Gardiner said, rolling his eyes to the ceiling and slouching in his chair. "Although at least the entertainment tonight isn't that awful quartet. She's found some psychic. Madame Palianko or Petroika or something equally Russian. You see my wife's foibles aren't just limited to her taste in music but they've somehow managed to venture into the Other World."

"Twaddle," Wentforth said between puffs.

"Caroline will be seeing spirits for weeks," Gardiner said, rolling his eyes. "Last time we had a medium over she was convinced the ghost of her Uncle Merryweather was trapped in the credenza."

"We don't love them for their minds, now do we?" Simon said.

Gardiner barked out a loud laugh. "No, indeed."

"They are pleasant company though," Simon said. "I'll admit my trip from New York has me rather lonely."

Gardiner's eyes lit up. "I'm sure. Perhaps I could make some introductions?"

"Do you know any young ladies who perhaps have just arrived in town?"

"That's an odd stipulation."

Simon swallowed the bile that crept up in the back of his throat. "I find young women new to a city are more...pliant."

"Very good," Gardiner growled appreciatively. "Hmm... I think I might just have the very girl for you."

"Really? And her name?" He didn't dare get his hopes up, but he could feel his heart begin to race at even the possibility.

Gardiner waved the question away. "What does it matter? Someone Caroline met. You'll come to the party and see for yourself. If she isn't to your taste I'm sure there are others that will suffice. I doubt you have trouble on that score. Being a baron and all!"

"Baronet," Simon corrected.

"Tonight then?" Gardiner asked.

Simon had little choice. He was in a city of nearly half a million people. Finding Elizabeth by wandering the streets was madness. He had to hope that San Francisco society was incestuous as every other he'd known and that eventually, he'd find her. "That's very generous of you."

Gardiner laughed, a high-pitched unpleasant sound. "We'll see if you still think so after the party."

MONIQUE MARTIN

Chapter Nine

T̲HE END OF M̲ARKET Street was chaos. Cable cars queued up in a turn of the century traffic jam as a growing throng of people gathered at the front of the Ferry Building. As she and Max got closer, she could hear a brass band belting out "Won't You Come Home, Bill Bailey?" from a small stage that was decorated with red, white and blue bunting. A handful of people sat in chairs at the back of the platform as the band entertained the growing crowd.

Just as it had in 1929 New York, Elizabeth was struck with how well dressed everyone was. Nearly every single one of the men wore a suit and a hat. Many of them were a bit grungy, but then the streets were half dirt and horses.

The women's dresses were all long, corsets tight and hats huge. Even the children that whizzed by with their penny candy and brightly colored pinwheels were miniature versions of the adults.

As much as Elizabeth loved to slob around in her jeans and t-shirt, the world had definitely lost something when it went casual. Her father had been a throwback. He never wore jeans. She didn't think he ever owned a pair. He had two suits, four shirts and two ties—one that was lucky and the one he was wearing.

The gentle pressure of Max's hand on her elbow pulled her out of the memory. "This way," he said.

The crowd was getting thicker as they neared the stage. "What's going on?"

"You wanted to meet Victor Graham, didn't you? He's the bulldog on the right," he said pointing to the back of the stage.

Elizabeth craned her neck to see him, but they were still too far back and she was far too short. Max took her arm and together they threaded their way toward the foot of the stage.

"What is all this?" Elizabeth yelled above the din.

"Graham throws a little party like this every time he buys something."

"What did he buy?"

"Cable Cars."

"All of them?"

"Almost," Max said and then, spotting someone ahead, he waved frantically. "Teddy!"

Max continued to lead her through the crowd until they finally emerged on the other side. Max and a small, nervous man with a neatly trimmed brown beard shook hands. The little man held a lunch-size brown paper sack tightly to his chest and worried a peanut like a chipmunk. Max clapped him on the back. "Should have known you'd be here, old man. Elizabeth West," Max said. "May I present Theodore Fiske. An old friend from school."

Teddy blushed beneath his whiskers and ducked his head.

Max leaned in and whispered to Elizabeth. "He's a bit shy."

Elizabeth extended her hand. "Nice to meet you, Mr. Fiske."

Teddy looked at her hand anxiously. He blinked nervously a few times then extended his peanut-filled hand. "Sorry. I…" he mumbled as he dropped the peanuts and rubbed his hand on the leg of his trousers. "Hello. Teddy. I mean to say, you can call me Teddy. I'll just…"

He bobbed his head as Elizabeth shook his hand. "Peanut?" he offered shoving the bag toward her.

Teddy wasn't just shy; he was…different.

"Teddy," Max scolded gently.

"I'd love one," Elizabeth said and dipped her hand into the offered bag. "And call me Elizabeth."

Teddy positively beamed at her with an endearing childlike quality that won her heart instantly and completely.

The band finished "Bill Bailey" and swung right into "Pomp & Circumstance". An attractive man in his early thirties moved to the front of the platform and waved to the crowd. They cheered loudly in response.

He was energy personified and reminded her of how Teddy Roosevelt must have looked when he was younger. He commanded the crowd with a confident ease.

"That's Graham," Max said.

Graham lifted his arms to silence the crowd. "Thank you. Thank you! Welcome to the future!"

That was met with a loud, frenetic round of applause from the audience. Graham milked it for a moment before asking for quiet again. "Just over fifty years ago, San Francisco was one dirt road and a thousand dreamers."

He surveyed the crowd. "Today, San Francisco is home to over a quarter of a million dreamers. That's progress, my friends!"

The crowd roared its approval. He was good.

"Electricity surges through this great city, lighting the way to the future thanks to great men like George Roe and Thomas Edison. That's progress! Messages can travel around the entire globe from our own Cliff House to the foreign shores of the Empire of Japan and back in minutes thanks to great men like John Mackay! That's progress! San Francisco is the greatest city in the greatest country in the world thanks to people like you! That's progress!"

The crowd went wild with applause, and despite not having any idea what was going, Elizabeth found herself joining in.

"I'm just a humble citizen. I don't claim to be in the company of these great men, but I am proud to be part of this great city. And proud to welcome the Market Street Railway into the Graham Transportation family. That's progress!"

It didn't make much sense, but the crowd didn't care.

"Consolidation! Better service! And that means potentially lower fares!"

"You mean lower wages!" a voice yelled out over the din.

Graham clearly heard the heckler, but did his best to ignore him and continue. "A more efficient company is a better company!"

"Is that what you told the twenty men you fired when you bought the last one?"

Elizabeth edged forward to get a better look at the heckler. He was small, but built like a bulldog with a face to match. Two larger men wearing gray coveralls and threadbare jackets flanked him on either side.

Graham apparently decided that he couldn't avoid the dissenter anymore. "During a merger there are hard decisions to be made."

"Lies! You made promises you didn't keep! Union shops, you said. Closed shops!"

A few others from the crowd started to grumble. The anger from the men was palpable. And dangerous.

"Lies are your progress!"

Elizabeth saw the man nearest to her reach inside his jacket. He was going for a weapon. She reacted instinctively. All she could think of was Simon as she ran toward the man.

"Gun!" she cried out as she closed in on him and lowered her shoulder. Her years of watching football under the Friday night lights in Texas had taught her what to do. Head up, shoulder down and drive through your man.

She did, but it was a bit like driving a Yugo through a brick wall. It was a good thing he was turning and slightly off balance when she crashed into him or she would have just bounced off.

As it was, they fell in a tangled heap onto the pavement. The big man under her was stunned and looked up at her with wild, blue eyes. The next minute was a blur of men grabbing men and Elizabeth being lifted off the ground.

"Are you all right?" Max said appearing at her side.

"He's got a gun!" Elizabeth said. "He was going to shoot Graham."

"I was not," the big man protested in a thick Swedish accent.

One of the men holding on to the gunmen, she realized, was a policemen. He reached inside the Swedes' jacket and pulled out what was left of a big red tomato. The gathered crowd laughed.

"Going to throw this, were you?" the policeman demanded.

"No!" the big Swede said. "It is my lunch!"

That won another round of laughter from the crowd.

"I was hungry."

Elizabeth's cheeks burned with embarrassment and she wondered if she wished hard enough that she could turn invisible.

"All right, all right," the policeman said. "Show's over." He waited for the crowd to ease back before he let go of the man and turned to the heckler. "All right, Ross, you and your men have made your point. Head out."

The man grunted, but nodded his head to his partners. "Let's go, boys."

"We wouldn't want any more," the policeman said as he tossed the Swede his smushed tomato, "vegetables hurt."

"It's actually technically a fruit," Teddy offered.

The policeman narrowed his eyes at Elizabeth. "Keep an eye out for carrots," he said before laughing and disappearing into the crowd.

"Dear lord, can we please leave?" Elizabeth asked quietly, wishing they were anywhere else.

"Not before you explain that," Max said. "It was…magnificent."

This was so humiliating. She could still feel the crowd's eyes on her. "Please?" she tried again.

"Wait there!" a voice called out. Graham jumped down from the stage. He tugged on the hem of his vest and smiled broadly. "I didn't get a chance to thank you, young lady."

Apparently invisibility by sheer will was a no go. "I'm sorry."

"Don't apologize," Graham said, half addressing her, but favoring the crowd. "You're quite the heroine! Risked your life for mine and for that I'm eternally grateful. I hope you'll join me for the banquet luncheon at the Cliff House later today as my personal guest."

The crowd applauded.

"This young woman is the very picture of progress." He put his arm tightly around Elizabeth's shoulders and turned her toward the crowd and, much to her eternal shame, a group of reporters.

"My heroine. My Tomato Girl!" he cried as the bright light from a photographer's flash-lamp exploded.

Chapter Ten

THE CLIFF HOUSE WAS built in the style of a 17th century French chateau, although the pediments were clearly 18th century. At least, according to Teddy Fiske, who wasn't just a font of information, he was a geyser.

When they'd arrived at the Cliff House grounds, Elizabeth had made an off-hand comment about one of the statues that lined the parapet. A brief, rambling and absolutely adorable lecture on the etymology of the word *parapet* followed. It started out well enough with Latin roots, *parare* and *pectus*, and ended with a furious blush as Teddy realized he'd accidentally said the word "breast".

This particular parapet was far from your typical battlement though. It was more like one of the elaborate gardens at San Simeon. Beautifully manicured lawns led to a long walled edge that overlooked the Cliff House and the rocky shore below. The wall was studded with Roman statues, vases and wrought iron chairs and a few people braved the cold ocean breeze to enjoy the view.

And it was an amazing view. From the cliff-side vista she could see for miles down the coast to the South or watch the tall ships sail in and out of the Golden Gate to the North. She couldn't see the bridge from there, but she reminded herself, she couldn't see the bridge from anywhere. It wouldn't be built for another thirty years or so.

A cluster of rocks just off the shore caught her eye. "Did that rock just…move?"

Max laughed. "Seals. You'll be able to see them better from the other side."

Elizabeth loved to watch the seals in Santa Barbara. After living landlocked in Texas for most of her life, she adored the movement and life of the ocean. It had been a pleasant surprise that Simon did too. He wasn't exactly the beachy sort. It was impossible to picture him in pair of Bermudas and flip-flops. He was more the cable knit sweater and Burberry pea coat type. It shouldn't have been all that shocking; after all, England is an island. Lots of water to be had.

The party was already well underway by the time they arrived. Graham's banquet took over the entirety of the third floor. Of course, there were seven stories to the Cliff House, so there was still plenty of room for everyone else.

The private section of the party, for only the chi-est of the chi-chi, was held in a special dining room overlooking the ocean. A few dozen four-top table were scattered through the long room with one larger table at one end and a player piano on steroids at the other. The brand new orchestrion was a band in a box. A big box. The size of a huge armoire it played scrolls of popular music. But it wasn't just a piano or an organ it had wind, string and percussion instruments. Its rendition of "Yankee Doodle Boy" was loud, bizarre and wonderful.

Max, Teddy and Elizabeth were seated in a place of honor near the main table. Graham was a genial host, working the room, while his wife sat solemnly at the table. She was young, probably in her mid-twenties and pretty, but she looked tired and drawn. She pushed her food around the plate making it look like she'd eaten more than she had. On Graham's other side was an older gentlemen with a pinched face and a mustache you could hang towels on.

"Who's that?" Elizabeth asked. "The man next to Graham?"

"That's the Admiral," Max said. "He owns the Cliff House."

"An admiral?"

"Not a real admiral," Max said. "He was in the Union Navy, but just as a cook on a sloop."

"Sloop of war," Teddy corrected as he arranged and rearranged his silverware.

"He's a self-made man and not a fan of your mister Graham. Who married," he said with a nod toward Mary Graham, "rather well."

Mary Graham looked a little like a hothouse flower with the heat up too high. So, Victor Graham had married her and inherited her family fortune. And apparently wasn't afraid to spend it.

"Adler, that's the Admiral," Max continued, "put in a bid for the Market Street Railway. He wanted to connect the ferries with his own section of the rail all the way here to Cliff House."

"But, Graham got the deal?"

"Graham always gets the deal."

The Admiral stood, giving Mrs. Graham a curt bow before walking over to the large bank of windows that overlooked the Pacific. He stood with one hand on the sill like it was the quarterdeck of a great ship. He looked like he might sail the whole darn continent into the West if he could.

The Admiral was obviously not a happy man. Losing the contract to Graham must have been bad enough, but for Graham to have his celebration party at the Cliff House was rubbing salt into the wound. Way to make an enemy, Victor. That made two that she knew of, the union workers and the Admiral. And, judging from the expression on Mrs. Graham's face, it might be three. How many enemies can one man have?

It was a good thing she knew roughly when the murder, scratch that, attempted murder was going to take place. Five days and counting—Easter Sunday. It would be impossible to stay with him every second of every day. As it was, she was going to have a hard enough time of it. Graham wasn't exactly the stay home and knit type, but, whatever it took, Elizabeth was going to save his life, and Simon's.

"You're looking very intense," Max said.

"Am I? I must need more champagne," Elizabeth said and then emptied her glass.

"For the Tomato Girl? Only the best," Max said as he waved to the waiter.

Elizabeth shook her head. What a mess she'd made of that. "That was so embarrassing."

"It was surprising," Max admitted.

Elizabeth dug into the dusty files in the very back of her brain for an excuse. "It was McKinley all over again. At least, I was afraid it was. I just…reacted."

"Were you there when it happened?"

Think, think, think. President McKinley had been assassinated by an anarchist at the Pan-American Exposition in 1901 in Buffalo, New York. She remembered that much, which she was pretty proud of, but it was hardly enough to spin a convincing lie. Luckily, the waiter came and refilled their water glasses buying her just enough to time to come up with a plausible story.

"No. I was at the exposition the day before, but it was still very difficult." She took out her handkerchief and held it to her mouth and fluttered eyelashes in a positively valiant attempt to ward off impending fake tears.

"I'm sorry, I didn't mean to upset you," Max said.

"Tell me about you," Elizabeth said, recovering too quickly, but desperate to veer the conversation away from her. "Where did you two go to school together?"

"Harvard. But it's not as impressive as it sounds. I was legacy, but our Mr. Fiske here is an actual genius," Max said.

Teddy giggled and waved his hand at Max. "No, no."

"Oh, but he is. Truly," Max said. "While I was off reciting Ovid and wearing dresses for the Pudding, Teddy was wasting his time studying physics. He's quite the inventor too."

"Really?" Elizabeth didn't know much about physics and didn't think having seen all three Back to the Futures would be all that helpful. She wracked her brain for something physics-y or inventory to say. "I don't suppose you know Thomas Edison?"

"Bastard," Teddy said and then gasped as he realized he'd said that aloud.

Elizabeth laughed. "I've heard worse. Worse about Edison too."

Teddy glanced at her and held her eye for just a split second. He smiled and looked down again. "I shouldn't speak ill of the man, but I worked with Nikolai Tesla and—"

"Tesla?" She knew that name. "Love his coils!"

Teddy laughed delightedly. "You… you've heard of them?"

"Yes. I don't know much about them, but maybe you can explain them to me sometime."

Teddy swallowed hard and nodded. "I'd…I'd like that."

"Oh dear," Max said with a dramatic sigh. "You've no idea what you've unleashed."

"And what was it you said about wearing dresses?"

Max barked out a loud laugh. "Yes, it's true. And I was lovely."

Teddy giggled again and nodded. "He was."

"Hasty Pudding. Were you studying theater?" Elizabeth asked Max. He was straight out of Central Casting for a leading man.

Max moved his champagne glass aimlessly around the table as he spoke. "Literature or something. I left school early and traveled.

Aunt Lillian calls me a gadabout who never finishes what he starts, but I like to think of myself as an adventurer. Amundsen, but with fewer polar bears and more hot toddies. I went to Tahiti, Morocco, Peru. Anywhere and everywhere I could. Fell in love…with automobiles and even raced a little—Paris to Amsterdam. As they say, it's not the destination, but the journey."

"He sent me a shrunken head from Peru," Max said as he aligned his water glass with his wine glass. "I buried it in the yard."

Elizabeth stifled a laugh and asked Max if he won the race.

"No," he said, the bright light in his eyes dimming just a little. "I didn't finish."

"Solitary pleasures are the leading cause of consumption today," Judge Philpot intoned ominously. "Needless depletion of the body's precious fluids causes frightening effects in men: Premature senility and dementia. And in a woman," he added with hardened gaze, "nymphomania."

Simon gripped the crystal tumbler of Scotch in his hand more tightly. So far he'd endured banal conversations, tedious entertainments and venomous gossip disguised as concern. But this particular form of idiocy was nearly more than he could stand.

"Rubbish," Simon said.

The Judge spluttered and harrumphed. "I beg your pardon."

Simon was more than ready to spar, but Gardiner laughed and clapped the Judge on the shoulder in a friendly gesture that was received as anything but. "I was talking about golf, old man. The solitary pleasures of golf."

Philpot grunted. "Fruitless labor. Also a vice."

Agnes Philpot, who would have been a pretty woman if her face hadn't been weathered by the storms her husband created, gently touched his arm. "Perhaps this isn't the place, Douglas. I—"

Philpot silenced her with a glare and she withdrew her hand. "I can think of no better place. For far too long we've remained silent about the deleterious effects of sexual corruption on our society. We must shine the light of purity and truth on them or they will never be abolished."

In a testimony to hypocrisy Gardiner chimed in, "So true. So true. Thank heaven for men like you keeping us on the straight and narrow."

The doctor swallowed Gardiner's pabulum with austere humility. "It's a burden we all must share."

Simon knew that if he continued with this conversation he'd undoubtedly say something he shouldn't. As loath as he was to stay, he had to endure it. Gardiner's female acquaintance still hadn't arrived.

Looking for any escape, Simon saw Mrs. Gardiner as she flitted about from servant to servant, nervously overseeing the party. He'd met her only briefly, but she reminded him so much of one of his aunts—desperate to impress and eager to please and married to a man for whom she could never do either. Simon excused himself and approached her.

"Mrs. Gardiner?"

She jumped at her name and then patted her chest with her kerchief. "Is anything wrong, Sir Simon? Canapé?" she asked, stopping a passing waiter.

"No, thank you. And please, no 'sir'. I'd rather not draw attention to it."

"Oh! Of course," she said as she dismissed the waiter with a wave and anxiously pulled her kerchief through her hand. "I do so hope you're enjoying yourself. I'm afraid the quartet isn't up to its usual standards. I think the violinist has the croup. Poor fellow."

Simon waited a moment to be sure she'd finished. He'd noticed with her, you could never be quite sure. "I wanted to thank you for allowing me to join you this evening on such short notice. It was very generous of you."

She put a hand to neck to cover a blush, clearly overwhelmed at the small compliment. "Thank you, Sir Si—Mr. Cross. Mr. Gardiner has many acquaintances," she said, her veil of frippery slipping for a moment as her eyes sought out her husband across the room. "But very few I'm so pleased to meet."

Simon didn't need to look. He knew exactly what she was talking about. Clearly, Gardiner didn't even attempt to hide his liaisons from his wife. There were a great many things Simon had no tolerance for and slowly but surely Gardiner was making his way to the top of that list.

"I can assure you, Mrs. Gardiner, the pleasure is mine. You are a consummate hostess."

She tittered nervously and waved the compliment away with swish of her kerchief. "I understand you've traveled from New York. Did you stay there long?" "Don't bore the man to death with your questions on his first night, Caroline," Gardiner said, appearing at their side. "Usually she doesn't do that until the third party."

Simon kept a tight rein on his impulse to put the man in his place and merely said, "I wasn't bored in the least."

"Ah, Cross, no wonder the ladies here can't keep their tongues from wagging about you. And speaking of the ladies, I think we know one who'd like to make your acquaintance. And vice versa, if you catch my drift."

Hope flared in Simon's chest. While he waited for Gardiner's mystery woman, he'd been besieged by the attentions of single women of marrying age and then some since the night had begun.

"You'll excuse me, Mr. Cross," Mrs. Gardiner said as she quickly primped, patting her hair and tucking her kerchief into her sleeve. "I see new guests I should attend to."

Simon bowed slightly. "Of course." He turned back to Gardiner impatiently. "Where is she? This new girl?"

"You are chomping at the bit, aren't you," Gardiner said as he draped an arm over Simon's shoulder. "Oh, she'll be here soon."

Simon shrugged out from under Gardiner's arm. "You said that she—"

"Oh, the entertainment's here," Gardiner said with mock enthusiasm. "Bully."

With a grand sigh he joined his wife at the door to greet their new guest.

"Madame Petrovka," Mrs. Gardiner gushed, "it's so wonderful to have you here. Please, come in."

Madame Petrovka was not what Simon had expected. He'd envisioned a little old lady wearing a babushka. But Madame Petrovka was no Madame Blavatsky. She was as elegantly dressed as any of the ladies at the party. She looked to be in her mid-forties. Her hair was black, almost aubergine, and was set off by startlingly pale violet eyes. She wasn't exactly beautiful, her features were too sharp, but she was striking.

Like most spiritualists and mediums Simon had met in his research, she carried herself with easy confidence seasoned with just enough humility to make her marks feel comfortable. And like most, she came with an accomplice, or as they liked to call them, an assistant. Hers was a small man named Stryker with a scarred chin and dull deep-set eyes.

At one time, Simon had actually considered following in Houdini's footsteps and exposing fraudulent spiritualists. During his early days in occult studies, he'd seen firsthand what their lies could do to a person. It struck a chord in him. Perhaps it was because his family was so adept at manipulation, but he felt a responsibility to try to protect the unsuspecting victims. It had been deeply shocking when Simon realized that they weren't just the impressionable, the fragile and the desperate; they were men and women, educated people, much like himself, who had a hole inside them that needed filling. Much like himself.

He'd studied their techniques and become quite skilled at seeing past the smoke and the mirrors. The tricks and the slight of hand weren't the crux of it though. A good psychic was a student of human nature, schooled in behavioral science as well as spiritualism. The key to any successful fraud is a willingness on the part of the victim. An astute spiritualist knows just what carrots to dangle and what buttons to push to achieve their end.

As Simon watched Madame Petrovka greet the party guests he recognized the signs. What others saw as casual introductions, he knew were quick assessments. She might be appearing to admire a broach, but she was fishing. Fishing for information and for players in her little mummer's farce. He knew that she was measuring each person, calculating their viability, observing them with the cool precision of Sherlock Holmes.

Holmes. That was a sad irony that Simon could never quite accept. How had the man who created the world's greatest detective been fooled by so many spiritualists? Doyle had famously been a great devotee of spiritualism, even to the point of obsession. How could such a critically thinking man be fooled? And with the very skills he'd imbued his great detective with—observation, knowledge and deduction. Holmes solved crimes in the same way a fraudulent psychic fooled their victim. Doyle's fascination was a testament to the power of spiritualism and the complex susceptibility of the victims.

Not that all mediums were frauds. After all, there are more things in heaven and earth, Horatio, than are dreamt of in your philosophy. He believed it was potentially possible for someone to have the gift of sight. He'd just never met anyone who did. But considering the things he had seen, the things he himself had done, he'd be a fool to think it wasn't at least possible.

When it was his turn to greet Madame Petrovka he could see the wheels turning beneath her raven hair as they shook hands. She took full measure of him in mere seconds and dismissed him just as quickly. The last thing a medium wants is an unbeliever. Nothing can put the brakes on a reading faster than the negative energy of a naysayer. Sadly, no matter how deeply he wanted to stop what was about to happen, he knew he'd be an instant outcast if he did. He needed to be a good little guest and politely watch the show.

Madame Petrovka held court in one of the salons of the Gardiner's large home. There would be no séance this evening just readings and if, according to Madame Petrovka, someone deeply sensitive were to be found, a demonstration of somnambulism.

She began with disarming small talk, all subtly probing for the most suggestible guest. Sadly, she had her choice. Spiritualism had become quite popular in the latter half of the last century. It had even made its way into the royal families of Europe and the wealthiest homes in America. Finding someone willing to suspend all common sense was far too easy a task.

"You are such a sensitive group," Madame Petrovka said with the merest hint of a Russian accent—another staple of so many frauds. "I am sure the spirits are feeling welcome as we speak. But I sense there is one here who has contacted the Other World before. Is there such a person here?"

Mrs. Gardiner shyly raised her hand. "I spoke to my dearly departed Uncle just a few months ago. In this very room as a matter of fact."

"Yes!" Madame Petrovka said loudly, eliciting delighted gasps from the crowd. "I can sense a presence."

Reginald Gardiner snorted. For once, Simon was inclined to agree with Gardiner, but he kept his expression neutral.

"Yes, he is here." She put a well-manicured hand to her temple and concentrated. "But, he doesn't feel welcome, I'm afraid. He did ask me to say goodbye to a Kitty."

Mrs. Gardiner gasped. "That's what he used to call me!" This was followed by a cooing chorus of delight. Simon was far less impressed. It would have been easy enough for Madame Petrovka to have paid the last psychic for a little inside information. Considering the vagueness of the remarks so far, it could have even been clever guesses.

As the evening wore on and Simon's patience wore thin, he noticed that Madame Petrovka wasn't a garden variety medium. She used a mixture of techniques ranging from Mesmerism to automatic writing to enthrall her audience. She tried to channel the spirit of a Revolutionary War hero distantly related to one of the guests, but, apparently, his wounds pained him too greatly.

Madame Petrovka was very good at what she did. She handled her audience masterfully, seeming to always know when to press on and when to retreat. Simon was impressed and worried. He tried to brush his concern aside as merely his distaste for her profession, but he couldn't shake the feeling that there was more to it than that.

She unnerved him. He wasn't easily frightened and certainly not prone to flights of fancy, but there was something about this woman that set his teeth on edge. He watched her through the night with equal parts curiosity and dread.

In the end, the performance was far from exceptional and the young woman who he was supposed to meet never arrived. Gardiner had made some excuse, but it turned out that it wouldn't have mattered. She wasn't Elizabeth. She was some red-headed second cousin of someone he couldn't remember.

That night as he rode in his carriage back to his hotel, his thoughts were of two women, the one he had to find and one he wished he hadn't.

CHAPTER ELEVEN

"**R**EALLY!"

Simon rubbed his temple and nursed his tea. Philpot was busy being affronted over something innocuous poor Livingston had said, while Gardiner gleefully watched the spectacle. It was the very definition of tiresome.

He reminded himself that it was only his second day there, but that didn't make this lot any more tolerable. He'd dutifully taken up his post in one of the reading chairs in Haven's club room subtly and not so subtly making enquiries about any young ladies that were new to town.

If the morning at the club didn't bear fruit, he'd spread his net wider. He'd already paid several bellboys and elevator operators a kingly sum to be his eyes and ears at the hotel. People in service and small children were the best spies. Most people ignored them and spoke freely about even the most personal things in their company.

A shoeshine boy worked like the devil in the far corner of the room. Maybe it was time to bring a few more into the fold.

Paperboys, shoeshine boys and street urchins were beneath most people's notice and could be invaluable additions to his network.

He'd already visited several dressmakers' shops. He knew Elizabeth would need clothes made. Time travelers, he'd learned, needed to travel light. Hopefully, one of the seamstresses would hear something about her. This afternoon, if he wasn't any closer to finding her, he was going to walk Nob Hill. Of course, that still left Russian Hill and a few other elite neighborhoods. It was a long shot, but he'd be damned if he was going to leave any stone unturned. The earthquake was just under a week away and they had to be out of the city by then.

Simon shifted in his seat, trying to shut out Gardiner's inane babble. He picked up a newspaper from the side table, unfolded it and stared in dumb silence at the front page. It took him a second to recover and when he did he let out a joyful laugh so loud that Wentforth dropped his pipe.

"Good lord man!" Gardiner squeaked. Simon waved him off and stared down at the grainy photograph emblazoned on the front page.

When he'd opened the paper, he'd fully expected to see more about the devastation left by Mount Vesuvius' eruption. The last thing he'd expected to find was a picture of Elizabeth. "Tomato girl," he said with a chuckle.

She was alive and well and, as he skimmed the story of her heroic rescue of Graham, in true Elizabeth form. How he'd missed her special brand of insanity. His heart beat faster at just the thought of being with her again. Knowing she was safe lifted the weight from his shoulders he'd carried with him since she'd stormed out. He would make amends; he would beg her forgiveness; he would make it all right again. Of course, he still had to find her first.

The paper didn't give many details. The story itself was short. There was a photograph of Graham and Elizabeth and an artist's rendering of the "tomato incident".

His relative solitude was interrupted by a loud hello shouted across the room. The man waved to someone and virtually jogged toward Simon's section of the room with self-assured idiocy. He reminded Simon of the dunderheaded athletes in his class who carried themselves with entitled nonchalance. Until he failed them, that is.

"So good of you to meet me, Mr. Roth. My aunt was sorry she missed you the other day."

"Good to see you, Maxwell."

Simon tried to tune them out, only listening for bits of information that might be useful. He'd become rather adept at eavesdropping, able to cull out snatches of conversation to follow up any possible leads later. This particular conversation consisted of what amounted to a plea for money for a charity. Something to do with a Mrs. Eldridge and the Chinese Mission.

"I'm sure something can be arranged," Roth said.

"Good. Aunt Lillian will be very pleased." The man flopped down into one of the club chairs and sighed.

"You seem to be in a very good mood, even for you," Roth said.

Maxwell stretched out his legs in front of him and slid down further into his chair. "I am. Have you seen the paper?"

"No."

"Do you mind?" Maxwell asked. It took Simon a moment to realize he was talking to him. "The paper? May I?"

Simon reluctantly handed it to him.

Max smiled down at the front page. "I never thought I'd say this, but I think I might have found the one." He handed Roth the paper.

"Since lightning didn't strike you dead on the very spot, I suppose you actually mean that this time."

"I think I just might. Isn't she lovely?"

"The Tomato Girl?"

Simon jolted upright. With more effort than he'd like to admit, he forced a veneer of calm over his features. "Do you know her?"

"Not as well as I'd like to," Harrington said. He quirked his head to the side like a small dog. "Do I know you?"

"Simon Cross."

Gardiner snatched the paper from Roth's hands. "Sir Simon, Harrington. Harrington, Cross. Oh, she is delightful, isn't she? And feisty too!"

Simon reined in his impulse to shove the paper down Gardiner's throat and instead looked at Harrington with what he hoped was a casual smile. "I don't suppose you know where she is? We're old friends and I'd love to say hello."

Simon forced himself to sit on the sofa. He couldn't exactly prowl the room or worse yet, throw open every door in the place until he found her. Even if that was exactly what he wanted to do. Elizabeth was here, nearly within his reach, and he was forced to sit and wait with Harrington of all people.

The very picture of nonchalant privilege, Harrington leaned back in his chair and stretched out his legs as he plucked off his driving gloves. "You know how women like to keep a man waiting," he said, as if they shared some common bond.

It was all Simon could do not to knock out some of his perfect teeth. The proprietary way he'd said Elizabeth's name when he'd instructed the butler to announce his arrival still chafed. Not Miss West, which would have been proper, but Elizabeth, implying an intimacy Simon did not want to consider. And not a word of his waxing on about how she was the one for him had faded from Simon's memory. All of that, however, would be dealt with swiftly and decisively, later. For now, the only thing Simon wanted was to see Elizabeth again.

The doorknob turned and Simon sprung to his feet ready to go to her. But it wasn't Elizabeth. An elderly woman entered and Harrington, all manners not completely deteriorated, managed to stand. "Good morning, Aunt Lillian," he said as he kissed her cheek.

Simon strained for a glimpse of Elizabeth behind her, but the hall was empty. Belatedly, he realized he was being introduced. Simon plastered on a courtly smile and gave a small deferential bow. "Mrs. Eldridge. I'm sorry for barging in like this."

Harrington leaned against the door jam. "Rank has its privileges."

"You'll forgive my nephew, Sir Simon. What he lacks in tact he more than makes up for in impudence. Won't you have a seat?"

"Thank you. I—"

The rest of the words were lost when Elizabeth, his Elizabeth, walked into the room. Simon's heart, like a cannon shell trapped in the breech, nearly exploded in his chest.

She playfully greeted Harrington and then, as she turned, she saw him. In the breadth of a few seconds her expression raced from disbelief to something he prayed was love. "Simon?"

He ignored the shock and heard only the hope. His voice was a rasp, rising from deep within his soul. "Elizabeth."

In a way he'd missed her more than he could have imagined. She smiled. Then, as she remembered their audience, she bridled her emotions, but like her, they were far from tamed and it took an effort to control them.

"What are you doing here?" she asked in a voice pressing far too hard on insouciance to be anything but the opposite.

Simon kept his eyes fixed on her, drinking in every aspect. "It's good to see you."

He could see her breath was short. Her chest rose and fell quickly and her cheeks were flushed.

"I've just arrived from New York. Imagine my surprise when I saw you in the paper."

Her blush spread to her neck, but she recovered quickly. "Looks like it's a day full of surprises."

"Isn't it?" Harrington said as he glared at Simon for a moment, before turning to Elizabeth. "Are you ready to go?"

"Be a good chap, won't you?" Simon said before Elizabeth could respond. There was no way on heaven or earth she was leaving his side now. "I'm sure you could spare her for the day, so two old friends might get reacquainted."

Judging from Harrington's reaction, Simon knew he had him trapped. Good manners were an underrated weapon.

"That's up to Elizabeth."

And damn her if she didn't think about it. What in God's name was there to think about?

Finally, she broke the silence. "Do you mind, Max?"

He was obviously crestfallen and Simon managed not to gloat. Too much.

"I'll make it up to you," she said, winning a smile from Harrington and a silent curse from Simon.

"Dinner tonight then? I've already made reservations, so you can't say no."

Elizabeth hesitated, but only for a moment. "That would be lovely."

Harrington grinned stupidly. "I'll fetch you around eight," he said and then cast a crowing smirk at Simon. "Cross."

Simon nodded his head in acknowledgement content to let him enjoy his false victory, after today that would be all he'd have.

Harrington left leaving Mrs. Eldridge standing awkwardly in what was obviously a private moment. The older woman looked at them with what Simon thought was envy, but whatever it was, it quickly fled. "I'm sure you two don't need me for this," she said and quietly closed the door behind her.

For a long moment, neither Simon nor Elizabeth moved. He could barely believe she was standing there before him. Flickers of emotion played upon her face—relief or anger—he didn't care which. He'd wanted only one thing for the last few days.

When she finally spoke her voice quavered as much as he feared his own would. "What are you doing here?"

All the speeches he'd rehearsed in the last few days didn't mean a damn thing. Now that he'd finally found her, there was only one thing wanted and words had nothing to do with it. With three quick steps he closed the distance between them, pulled her into his arms and kissed her with all of his heart.

Fierce desire and tender affection blended together in that kiss. The feel of her in his arms set all that was wrong to right again. The nights filled with longing and misery vanished. He pulled her body against his, not daring to let go.

After a long moment he pulled back. "That," he said, "is what I'm doing here."

Chapter Twelve

Elizabeth stood frozen, trapped between wanting to fall into his arms and wanting to sock him right in the nose for everything he'd made her go through. He'd been a colossal ass, but he'd also fought through time and space to be by her side. Seeing him again and kissing him had addled her brains a little, but not completely.

"Don't think we're not going to have a serious talk about you know what," she said.

He stared at her expectantly torn between fear and hope. It was a stark reminder. That very dichotomy was one of the reasons she loved him so much. He was a collision of opposites. The cool, so very British exterior that hid the most passionate man she'd ever known. He could recite Chaucer and quote Monty Python. He shut out the world and let her in.

"But right now," she continued, reaching up to caress his cheek. "I think you'd better kiss me again."

He gladly obliged. "God, I missed you," he whispered in a voice rough and tender with emotion.

She rested her head on his chest for a moment, content to let everything that was and everything that would be disappear. She'd been so intent on doing everything alone, she'd forgotten what a gift it was not to have to.

Simon kissed the crown of her head and she felt as much as heard his sigh of relief. In the days since she'd arrived, she'd spent so much time angry about what had happened, she'd forgotten even to consider what he must have been going through. She eased back and one glance at his face told her the story of hardship, worry and desperation he'd endured. No matter how often she saw it in his eyes, or heard him whisper it to her in the dark, she was always awed by the sheer power of his love. The stoic, impenetrable Simon Cross laid bare and offered his heart to her again and again.

The lump in her throat grew to guava-size and the glistening around the edges of Simon's eyes told her they were both on shaky ground. And Mrs. Eldridge's parlor was no place for an emotional scene. Gerald wouldn't approve.

Clearing her throat, she managed a smile. "What took you so long?"

Simon laughed with that deep, rich resonate sound that found its way straight into her soul. He really needed to laugh more often.

He matched her smile, but his eyes gave him away.

"I'm glad you're here," she said. And then she noticed a small bruise on the edge of his jaw. "What happened?"

She touched his cheek and he took her hand and kissed her palm. "It's nothing."

The final burden seemingly lifted from his shoulders, he let out a deep breath and gently tucked a stray tendril of hair behind her ear. With as much tenderness as he'd had passion a few moments ago, his gaze caressed her face. His long fingers traced the edge of her jaw.

Elizabeth closed her eyes and leaned into his hand.

"Are you all right?" he asked.

"Much better now." She took his hand and led him to the sofa. She stared at him for a long moment before looking down. "I never thought you'd…"

Simon tilted her chin up. "I will *always* come for you."

Her heart fluttered in her chest. Love's arrhythmia. "What made you change your mind?"

Simon frowned and his eyes darted from side to side like they did when he was searching for the right words. Giving her a wan smile, he shook his head. He walked to the window and stared out into the yard before turning back to her. "I should have listened. I'm still not ready to trust the Council, but I should have trusted you. But I…was angry and if I'm honest, I was afraid."

"I know it's hard."

He shook his head. "I'm not sure you really know how difficult it is for me. I never thought I'd fall in love. I certainly never thought I'd fall in love with someone like you."

She smiled wryly. "Thanks a lot."

Simon ran a hand through his hair and rubbed the back of his neck. "You'd think after nearly twenty years of teaching I'd learn how to say what I want to say."

"You don't have to say anything." She crossed the room to stand next to him. He always looked so lost when he tried to make amends.

"For five days, I've been thinking about what I was going to say when I found you. And now that I have, every word has fled me," he said with a sad smile.

She stepped toward him and cupped the side of his face. "Simon."

He closed his eyes for a moment and then sighed. "I can't promise that I'll always be the man you deserve, but I can promise that I'll always try to be."

Elizabeth felt tears welling in her eyes.

"When you came to me about the Council. I reacted badly. I'm sorry. I should have told you the day they came to me." He took both of her hands in his. "I need you to know something, Elizabeth. I need you to know that I will always support you. No matter how reckless and insane your ideas may be."

"And there's my Simon," Elizabeth said with a laugh.

"And yours for the taking."

She kissed him again. "Consider yourself took."

San Francisco was the poster child for growing America. Brash, striving and never satisfied, it embodied the spirit of a nation feeling its oats. From President Teddy Roosevelt to the newest immigrant to land on its shores, America was in vigorous pursuit of greatness. Always bold, often blundering, and seldom tactful, America was reaching for the brass ring with both hands.

Full of growing pains and beautiful mistakes, San Francisco was a teenage city ready to bust out. The population had grown from a mere 500 before the gold rush of 1849 to close to half a million by the turn of the century. What had been little more than pastures and mining towns was now a cosmopolitan city with thriving industry, modern technology and more money than you could shake a stick at. Empire building was its favorite pastime.

At the city's heart, Market Street was packed with every possible conveyance known to man. Horse drawn carts and carriages parried with a few boisterous automobiles and bulky cable cars. Pedestrians and cyclists wove in and out of the mess at will. If there were laws of the road, no one obeyed them.

"Be careful," Simon said as he tugged on Elizabeth's elbow, pulling her back and keeping her from being run over by a low-slung drayage cart.

Elizabeth sheepishly smiled her thanks. She'd been so caught up in the spectacle, she wasn't paying close enough attention. It was only her second time travel experience, after all, she was allowed to gape a little.

She knew Simon didn't quite share her enthusiasm for the adventure of it all. What she saw as wondrous, he saw as potentially dangerous. And that was the rub, wasn't it? That, in part at least, is what had split them apart.

She was bound and determined that it wouldn't keep them apart though. Simon was, deep in his heart, an explorer too. He might have preferred to do it from the safety of a leather wingback chair and risk only paper cuts, but his mind was as inquisitive as hers. She just needed to give it a little nudge.

And, if she were honest with herself, she liked the feeling of his protective presence. If it could always be like it was now, like the reassuring feeling of his hand lightly holding her arm. Not guiding her, not holding back, just being at her side.

She and Simon had left Mrs. Eldridge's to go for a walk and ended up, as apparently did everyone else in the city, on Market Street. As they walked they'd caught each other up on their adventures so far. While his description was concise and on point, very Joe Friday, hers was long, rambling and would have been bound in several volumes.

The most maddening part was that he didn't seem to be as worried as she was, or frankly at all, about the consequences if they failed. You'd think not existing would be troubling, but he didn't seem bothered. That was, she supposed, one of the perks of thinking the Council was full of beans. He considered the whole thing a wild goose chase, but had learned enough not to repeatedly point that out.

He was quick, however, to point out that getting her face plastered all over the biggest newspaper in San Francisco wasn't exactly time travel etiquette. Not that he could really be angry with her for it. It was, as he put it, quintessentially Elizabeth, and without it he might not have found her so quickly.

With only four days until the attempt on Graham's life, they needed to learn more about who might want him dead. That meant finding out more about the Admiral and the union workers who'd protested his speech. Failing that Elizabeth was going to have herself surgically implanted to Graham's side.

A horse cart clattered past followed closely by a buzzing handful of flies and Elizabeth squinted up into the afternoon sun. It was an unseasonably warm spring day. Add to that an endless supply of dust and Elizabeth, as they said back home in Texas, was mighty parched.

Over the din of the traffic, Elizabeth heard the tempting gurgling sound of water. It appeared to be coming from a large bronze obelisky type thingy. It was a bit like a streetlamp on steroids that had large lion heads growing out of its base. And out of those lion heads streamed fresh, at least she hoped it was fresh, water.

"Now that's a drinking fountain," Elizabeth said as she started to lean over to take a swig.

"Elizabeth," Simon said with a scowl and a shake of his head.

"What? I'm thirsty?"

"You are also a lady. Theoretically," he added winning pursed lips from Elizabeth. Simon merely arched an eyebrow in response and continued, "Wouldn't you rather have a nice cold lemonade or a martini?"

"Is the Pope Catholic?"

"Really, Elizabeth."

She gave him a cheeky grin.

He sighed and gestured to an enormous building across the street. "My hotel."

"Why, Mr. Cross! If I didn't know better, I'd think you'd brought me here on purpose."

It was his turn to grin and Elizabeth couldn't help but laugh. How she loved that smile. It made all sorts of promises she couldn't wait to collect on.

"As big as Hell and half of Texas," Elizabeth whispered to herself as they entered the Palace Hotel's Grand Court.

Simon approached the front desk and asked for his room key. The clerk quickly obliged and Simon led Elizabeth to one of the "rising rooms" as they called them. The elevator was a little unsteady as it inched its way up to the sixth floor. It gave one last lurch and bumped to a stop. Elizabeth gripped Simon's arm.

He smiled down at her. "You get used to it."

When they reached Simon's room, Elizabeth hesitated. "I'm not sure this is…proper."

Simon keyed the door open and turned to her, leaning in close. "I'm sure it isn't."

The late afternoon sun was just starting to dip behind the buildings and hills of Market Street. In the coming sunset even red brick looked hewn out of gold.

"It's incredible," Elizabeth said as she stood at the window and pulled the sheet tightly around her body. They'd made love and washed away the sins of the past week in the process. "I had no idea the city was so big already."

She didn't need to look to know that Simon wasn't enjoying the view, at least not the same one she was. She could feel him watching her. Finally, she turned to face him. He'd already dressed, mostly. He was barefoot and his starched white shirt was still undone. Her button-down professor was damn sexy when he was unbuttoned. For her part, she was going to enjoy her unfettered, beneath-the-sheet nakedness as long as possible.

He started to say something, but stopped. Instead, he reached out and caressed the edge of her jaw with back of his fingers. The way he looked at her always made her stomach drop, but this time there was more to it. It was so tender, so happy; it made her heart ache.

"I missed you too," she said.

He nodded and she could see the muscles of his jaw clench briefly. Taking pity on both of them, she stepped into his arms.

They just held each other for a minute. And in that minute, they could have been anywhere or anywhen and it wouldn't have mattered as long as they were together. That was a truth Elizabeth clung to.

Simon eased back a little and looked into her eyes. He held them for a moment before tilting his head down and capturing her mouth in a kiss. It was soft and gentle, like a first kiss.

It was a tiny spark at first, but it grew quickly. Elizabeth could feel it well up inside of her and she pulled Simon closer as she deepened the kiss. Simon's arms wound around her waist and pushed her body against his. He sat down in one of the large overstuffed chairs and pulled her down onto his lap.

She reached behind him to move his jacket from the chair, but it felt oddly heavy. She reached into his coat pocket and pulled out a pistol.

"What's this?" she said.

He took it from her hand and placed it on the end table. "A gun," he said and leaned in to kiss her neck.

"Simon! You know how I feel about guns."

"And you know how I feel about you. And if you don't, let me show you," he added as he pulled her closer. "Again."

He kissed her soundly and any reply was quickly forgotten. A knock at the door ruined the moment.

"Bugger."

"I'll get it," Elizabeth said as she slipped off his lap, picked up her sheet train and started for the door.

"Very funny." Simon grabbed her arm and nudged her to the bedroom. With a frown, she hid in the hall and peeked around the corner. The bellboy kept his eyes to himself as he placed their drink tray down on a table. Simon fished into his pocket, tipped the boy and hurried him out.

"Where were we?" he said.

"You were going to show me something…again," Elizabeth said with a wink.

"That's right," Simon said and handed Elizabeth her drink. "Cheers. I could order some food, if you'd like."

Elizabeth winced at that. "I'm having dinner with Max later, remember?"

Simon grunted. "Ah, yes. About your date—"

"It's not a date, Simon, and you know it. Max *is* a nice guy."

"Have you forgotten the last time you went out to dinner with a 'nice' guy?"

She hadn't forgotten. You don't forget a dinner with a vampire. Ever. But she wasn't going to rise to the bait. "Max is a nice guy," she repeated. "And yes, while technically they might be dates, to me their strictly mission-related outings."

She raised her chin high and tried to look mighty. It was a bit of stretch to pull off haughty though while wrapped in a king sized bed sheet. "I see."

She was about to give him what-for when she noticed the edge of his mouth quiver. He was trying not to laugh. He was toying with her.

"Very funny," she said.

Simon took another sip of his drink. He was maddening when he was calm. "I trust you."

"Then you don't mind?" Elizabeth said skeptically.

"I didn't say that."

Elizabeth huffed out a breath and plopped into a chair. "Simon-"

"Elizabeth," Simon said simply. "I trust you. You know that. Harrington is another matter."

"He's not going to try anything tonight."

"No, he isn't."

"You sound awfully sure of that," Elizabeth said.

"I am." Simon took another sip of his drink. "I'm going with you."

"Oh, Simon. I don't think—"

He put his glass down and stood up. "Don't think," he said holding his hand out to her and pulling her up and into his arms. He leaned down and kissed the side of her neck. "We've both done enough thinking."

He trailed kisses down her neck and with one fluid movement undid the loose knot she'd used to tie the sheet around her. It fell to the floor at their feet.

He scooped her up and into his arms. "Thinking's definitely overrated."

CHAPTER THIRTEEN

MAX OBVIOUSLY HADN'T BEEN pleased with the new arrangement for dinner, but he was too much of a gentleman to make a scene. Of course, that didn't stop him from taking a few corners too sharply and sending Simon sliding dangerously across the back seat of his car. Elizabeth had even seen Max smile to himself when he'd heard Simon's epithets after they hit a particularly deep pothole.

It was a hair-raising ride as usual, but they made it to the Poodle Dog restaurant in one piece. As Simon extricated himself from the backseat, his expression signaled that tropical depression Simon had been upgraded to tropical storm.

Elizabeth patted his arm gently and straightened the collar of his jacket. "Please, Simon," she whispered.

No matter how much Simon hated it, they couldn't afford to alienate someone like Max. He was their golden ticket through just about every door in town.

Simon grunted, but she could see his eyes soften.

The Poodle Dog restaurant was housed in a large six-story brick building. On the outside it was non-descript, but inside it was rococo gone loco. The large dining room had dozens of lavishly laid tables. The walls were covered with rich embroidered silks. Venetian glass chandeliers hung low from the gilded ceiling. And the chairs looked like they might get up and walk out on their thick, curved legs. It was wonderfully ridiculous. A lot like her three-way date, thought Elizabeth.

Both Simon and Max reached to pull her chair out for her. Each man held tightly onto his side of the chair and glared at the other. Elizabeth stood in no-man's land until the maître d' came to her rescue, clearing his throat and slipping between the two men.

"Mademoiselle."

"Thank you," she said with a glance at Simon and Max that held a healthy dose of "snap out of it."

Simon grumbled something about the French and Max frowned, but they both released the chair and took their seats with all the grace of two schoolboys who'd just had their knuckles rapped. The maître d' handed them the menus and when it came to the wine list, he held it out and raised a questioning eyebrow.

Max snatched it from his hand. "Please," he said, cutting off Simon's protest. "You're my guest."

Simon's manners hadn't completely dissolved. That and a quick kick in the shin under the table brought a tight smile and deferring nod.

Max gave the list a quick scan before handing it back. "Château Mouton Rothschild, '78."

Simon gave a quiet, but not too quiet "humph". If Max heard the disdain in it, he ignored it and turned his attention back to Elizabeth. And the game was on.

"So, Cross," Max said with an easygoing smile. "You don't mind if we dispense with the title, do you? This is America after all."

Elizabeth nearly blurted out, "What title?" but managed to stop herself. He would be explaining that later.

"Of course," Simon said to Max. "If it makes you uncomfortable."

Max's lips quivered with the strain of keeping his casual smile in place. "I understand you're here from New York. What brings you to our fair city?"

Simon cast a quick, but meaningful glance at Elizabeth before answering. "Business."

"What sort?"

Elizabeth had a flash of panic, but Simon answered smoothly. "Lloyds."

"Insurance?" Max said with a relieved smile. Any tension he'd had slipped away.

"And investments," Simon added.

Max turned to Elizabeth, effectively dismissing Simon. "I'm sure it's fascinating."

Simon's expression was enigmatic. "At times. Regardless, I hope to conclude my business here quickly," he said with a glance at Elizabeth.

"If there's anything I can do to hurry it along, old man," Max added. "Don't hesitate to ask."

"Very kind of you," Simon said flatly.

"I have to admit I find most business rather tedious," Max said as the waiter returned with their wine. "Life's too short to spend it sitting behind a desk. Did you know that there are tribes of Negro half-men, barely the size of a child, in the darkest jungles of Africa. And legends of gold beyond your wildest imaginings in the hidden tombs of the Pharaohs of Egypt."

Simon coughed and nearly choked on the wine. They'd both had their share of the "Kings" of Egypt during their last adventure. Elizabeth cast Simon a pleading glance.

"I'm sure it's fascinating," Simon said in a voice so dry it could have been vermouth.

"It is," Max said earnestly, missing the barb. "Of course, it's not for everyone. The world needs bankers and insurance salesmen. No offense, old man. But for some..." he said as he turned to Elizabeth. "That's not enough, is it?"

Elizabeth ignored the question, knowing any answer would lead to a path she'd rather not go down. "Max is planning on racing his car from Paris to..."

"Peking to Paris, actually."

"Right. Peking to Paris. Isn't that interesting, Simon?"

"Fascinating."

The conversation ground to a fine-grained halt. Apparently, in some cases, silence was more awkward than golden. Simon's last jab had ended the round and left both men sitting in their corners prepping for the next. Before the bell could ring, Elizabeth jumped into the fray.

"Simon has travelled quite a bit himself," Elizabeth said quickly.

Simon narrowed his eyes, but caught her expression. She wasn't going to put up with much more. Just a peek of her pique seemed to do the trick and he leaned back in his chair. "Europe and Asia, primarily. Good experience for a boy."

Max chuckled at that and leaned back in his chair to mirror Simon.

Elizabeth sighed quietly. Men. "I haven't traveled much."

It was true enough, a little time travel not withstanding. She'd seen a few states, but had never even left the country. The closest she'd come was a border town in Texas on a prom night best forgotten.

"You've traveled across America. That's more than most," Max said. "I'm amazed the men of New York let you leave, actually. However, their loss is my most pleasant gain."

Elizabeth blushed and thought she could actually see a puff of steam come out of Simon's ears.

The waiter came just in the nick of time to ward off any biting reply Simon might have been about to make. Whatever it was, he washed it down with a half glass of fine wine.

Once they'd placed their orders, the awkward silence returned.

"So, Cross," Max said draining his own glass. "How do you know our dear Elizabeth?"

"Dear Elizabeth," he said between clenched teeth and a tight smile. "Old family friend."

"Did you go to school with her father?" Max said. Elizabeth saw Simon's jaw clench at the dig. "I'd very much like to meet him some day."

Elizabeth's chest tightened the way it always did when someone reminded her that she'd never see her father again. Everyone said the feeling would fade away in time. She was still waiting.

"I didn't have the honor of knowing Elizabeth's father," Simon said. "I very much wish that I had."

That made Elizabeth smile. Her father and Simon couldn't have been more different. And yet, she knew they would have somehow gotten along. What she wouldn't give to have seen them meet for the first time.

"My father passed away," Elizabeth explained for Max's benefit.

"I didn't realize," Max said, but she waved away his apology.

"It's all right. Both of my parents are gone. I'm the last of my kind."

"A rare and beautiful thing. Just what every adventurer hopes to find," Max said as took hold of her hand brushed a light kiss across her knuckles. "Treasure."

Elizabeth felt a blush steal up her cheeks and took a quick sip of water. "Fool's gold."

"Hardly. Isn't she lovely when she's embarrassed?" Max said with a smile. "I think I could grow quite used to seeing that."

"Really?" Simon said casually. Or at least it sounded casual to the uninitiated. Elizabeth knew better. And that was definitely steam.

Oblivious, Max continued on. "What man wouldn't? Surely, you have no shortage of suitors back home."

Elizabeth stole a quick glance at Simon. "It's complicated."

"A beautiful and charming woman like you. How complicated can it be?"

Elizabeth fiddled with the collar of her blouse and resisted the urge to look at Simon. "You'd be surprised."

"New York must be filled with blind men and idiots. Present company excepted, of course," Max said with a nod toward Simon. "You should be proposed to regularly. In fact, I may take it upon myself to remedy the situation."

Elizabeth laughed. Simon did not.

The rest of dinner was a mixture of tense and tenser. Max was either unaware, didn't care or enjoyed discomfiting Simon. Whatever his reason, he continued to court Elizabeth subtly and not so subtly through the entire meal. Maybe Simon was right. It looked like to Max, their outings had been dates.

Elizabeth tried to steer the conversation to safer ground. She asked about Max's mother, his car, anything to keep him and Simon from sparring.

Finally, blessedly, the dinner ended. Now, she just needed to get this party train back to the station with as little blood spilled as possible.

When they arrived back at Mrs. Eldridge's house the tension was as thick as the evening fog. The two men escorted her to the front door. Max took her hand and kissed it as he bowed, bidding her goodnight.

Simon kept his distance and stared at her for a long moment. His expression said everything he couldn't. He bowed curtly and headed back down the walk without so much as a word.

She wanted to call out to him, to invite him inside. But judging from his body language, he needed some time to unwind. He was cranky, and she could hardly blame him. If their positions had been reversed, the cat would have had claws. As they say, tomorrow was another day. And, she guessed from the milkman's wagon that clattered down the street, only a few hours away.

"Give you a lift, old man?" Max said to Simon.

"No, thank you."

Max shrugged and started up his car. With a loud backfire that cut into the quiet, he drove off.

"Goodnight, Simon," Elizabeth said.

Simon lingered at the end of the walk for a long moment. He looked like he was about to say something when he mumbled a goodnight, stuffed his hands into his pockets and headed off into the cold night.

Elizabeth undressed and slipped into her silk nightgown, which was actually fancier than any dress she'd ever owned. She hated sleeping in something she was afraid to wrinkle. The floor was chilly under her feet as she walked across the room to close the heavy drapes. She had a beautiful view of the side garden. The moon hung just over the large Magnolia tree that stood sentinel in the side yard. Oversized white blossoms caught the moonlight.

Something tinked against the glass of her window and made her jump. The hell? There it was again. She peered out into the darkness and saw a shadowy figure step out from under the Magnolia tree. There was no mistaking who it was—Simon.

Quickly, she undid the window lock and raised the lower sash. An absurd image of him holding a boombox over his head as a

Peter Gabriel song played flashed into her mind. Of course, in this case it would probably be a Victrola playing Rachmaninoff.

She started to call out to him, but realized how late it was and waved a hand indicating that he should wait there.

As quickly and as quietly as she could, she made her way down stairs and slipped out the side door. She hurried across the cold, dewy grass.

"What are you doing here?" she asked.

"About bloody time. I've thrown half the rocks in the yard."

"Is something wrong?"

He shook his head and reached out to tuck a stray lock of hair behind her ear. "No," he said a bit hoarsely. "No. I just…" His voice trailed off and he shook his head again.

His strong hands held her arms and pulled her into his embrace. His arms circled her and held her to his chest. His clothes were chilled and damp from the night air. She could feel as much as hear his deep sigh.

When they pulled apart, Elizabeth rested her hands against his chest. He looked at her in that way that always made her heart skip a beat—tender, intense, absolute.

Elizabeth felt a surge of guilt. She knew she'd made the right decision. He could have come with her and chose not to. And yet…

"I'm not going anywhere," she said as she leaned into his warmth. Simon was always warm. Her own personal heater.

"Yes, you are," he said covering her hand with both of his. "Back inside, your hands are ice cold."

Elizabeth hesitated for a moment and then said, "Come with me."

Simon shook his head. "I should go. I just needed to see you again."

She spread out her arms in display. "Behold the Elizabeth."

Simon chuckled, but it faded quickly. "There is one favor I'd like to ask though. Harrington."

"He's harmless."

"But you're not."

"Me?" She hadn't done anything. What on earth was he talking about?

"He's falling in love with you."

Elizabeth waved her hand dismissively. "It's been two days."

Simon shrugged. "You're potent."

It took her a second to realize that Simon was completely serious. "He's just flirting." A lot.

"Perhaps," Simon said. "And if he isn't?" He let the question hang in the air between them.

"Then I'm being unfair to him, aren't I? Because there's only one man I love. Only one man I'll ever love."

Simon nodded almost imperceptibly.

"That's you, by the way."

She smothered his smile with another kiss.

His hand came up to cup her cheek and he pulled back. "You're freezing. You should go inside," Simon said rubbing her arms gently.

"Come with me." She wanted him. She wanted to wake up next him again.

Simon smiled. "I don't think Gerald would approve," he said with a nod of his head toward the side door.

Standing in the shadow of the doorway was Gerald, arms crossed tightly over his chest.

Elizabeth had to laugh. "He's just looking out for me. He means well."

"In that case, give him my thanks."

"He'll love that," she said with a laugh.

Simon turned her slightly to obscure Gerald's view, then caressed her cheek gently and kissed her once more. "Goodnight, love."

But he didn't let go and she didn't want him to. She could see his struggle and, despite what he'd said, she wasn't sure he could let her go. Unless she wanted to spend the night standing out here in her shift, it was up to her. She savored the last bit of his warmth and eased back out of his arms.

"I'll see you tomorrow," Elizabeth said, letting her hand linger on his chest. "Just the two of us this time. I promise."

"I'm going to hold you to that."

Elizabeth gave him a sly little smile. "I hope you do."

His eyes narrowed and she thought she heard him groan. "Goodnight, Simon," she said and then walked back across the lawn to the door and past a scowling Gerald.

"Goodnight, Gerald," she said without pause or explanation. She started up the back stairs but heard him grumble, "Englishmen."

CHAPTER FOURTEEN

"I HATE YOU," ELIZABETH SAID.

The corset didn't reply. She hadn't wanted to call the maid for help and nearly dislocated her shoulder tightening the laces herself. It was a cruel trick to keep women needy, she thought. Someone who can't even get dressed by themselves is bound to rely on others for everything. Suffrage couldn't come too soon.

She was just opening her door when Jane, the young maid of the house, scurried up to her.

"Good day, Miss," she said bobbing in a quick curtsy. "Mr. Foster was looking for you."

Gerald. She had a sinking feeling he was going to give her a lecture about what proper ladies did and didn't do including meeting men in the middle of the night in nothing but their shifts.

He might have been the butler, but he was the lord of the manor in every other way. Mrs. Eldridge had even assured her that she and Gerald had no secrets from each other.

"Where is he?"

"He's in his rooms, Miss. I was just bringing him these," she said holding out a stack of neatly folded laundry.

"I'll take them."

"But, Miss—"

"His rooms are upstairs?"

"Yes, Miss, first on the right, but—"

Elizabeth took the laundry. "Thank you, Jane."

She started up the stairs and suddenly felt like she was going to the principal's office or worse yet, her father's room for a serious talking to. She knocked on his door.

"Come."

Elizabeth opened the door and peeked inside. The room was fairly simple and Spartan, except for a portrait of President Roosevelt that hung above a small desk. Gerald sat on the edge of his bed, one trouser leg rolled up to his thigh. The stump of what had been his right leg poked out like a red, pinched and angry face.

She'd noticed his limp before, but it had never occurred to her that he might be…this. Whatever injury had caused the amputation had long since healed, but the end of it still looked raw and painful. She tried not to stare it at, but the harder she tried the more magnetic it became.

"I'm sorry," Elizabeth said.

Gerald looked up and his expression darkened. He stood on his one good leg and glared at her, his face turning a dark ruddy red. "What are you doing here? Don't they teach manners when you come from?"

"I'm sorry," Elizabeth said again. She held out the laundry. "Jane was bringing these and…please, sit down."

Trying not to look at his leg, she set the laundry down on the bed next to him. She didn't know what to say or where to look. "I didn't mean to intrude. Jane said you were looking for me."

When she noticed the lotions and fresh stockings, she mumbled another apology and started for the door. He'd obviously been tending to his leg when she came in.

"Do you always barge in where you're not welcome?"

Elizabeth turned back and answered without thinking. "Yes. At least that's what people tell me."

Gerald glared at her. Even in this state, he was an imposing man. His red hair seemed to grow a brighter shade with his anger. And then, slowly, the hard line of his mouth quivered and the corners turned up in a smile. Finally, a deep, booming laugh escaped. It was a wonderful sound, rich and deep and from the heart.

"Good. I like an honest woman."

"And I like a forgiving man," she said.

He laughed again, but this time there was no joy it. "I'm hardly that."

"Well, you haven't thrown me out."

"Yet," he said, but she could see the smile in his eyes. He gestured to a chair by the bed. "Are you going to sit or do I have to keep standing on my one good leg forever?"

Elizabeth sat down so quickly she nearly missed the chair. The room wasn't as impersonal as she'd first thought. A few small photographs sat in silver frames on a dresser and there were lots and lots of books.

She could feel him staring at her. She was trying not to look at his leg, but her eyes kept falling on it. The tip of it poked out from his pant leg. "Does it hurt much?"

"Some days." He picked up his prosthetic leg and turned it over in his hands. It looked heavy and had a large leather thigh brace, sort of like a corset for the upper-leg with thick laces and steel joints. Just below the knee there was a hollow wooden calf with a semi-articulated rubber foot. "Better than the alternative."

He put the leg down on the bed. "Getting a Winkley next time. This one's starting to chafe."

"I'm sorry."

"Unless you were manning a British cannon at Stoney Creek, you don't have anything to be sorry for," he said as he rolled down his pant leg. "But you don't want to hear about that."

She did. But she wasn't sure he wanted to tell her. In an attempt to change the topic, she blurted out, "Last night wasn't what you thought it was."

If he was surprised by the sudden change in topic, he didn't show it. "Wasn't it?"

"Okay, it was." She hadn't done anything to apologize for. What she did was her business after all. "I just don't want you to think I'm some kind of floozy."

"You don't need to explain yourself to me, girl."

She didn't and yet, she wanted to. She had no reason for it, but she wanted Gerald to understand. He was a curmudgeon, difficult to read and never what she expected. But, she liked him. He was one of those men who didn't give his approval easily and so it meant all the more when you earned it.

"I know," she said. "I have issues." When it was clear he had no idea what that meant, she quickly added, "Missing parts, you know, little emotional scars."

Gerald stared at her for a long moment seeming to see right into her soul. "Some wounds never heal. You just learn to live with them."

Elizabeth was suddenly embarrassed at how painfully transparent she was. "Jane said you were looking for me."

"A messenger came this morning with an invitation for you."

"Who's it from?"

"I don't read other people's mail." He picked up one of the stockings and started to dress his leg. Apparently, he was finished with her. She sat there like a dope for a moment waiting for what she didn't know and then finally stood.

"Thank you." She opened the door and started to leave, but his voice stopped her.

"I don't, by the way."

"Don't what?"

"Think you're a floozy," he said with a hint of a smile. "Not that it matters."

She smiled back. "It matters a little."

The invitation was from Victor Graham. She and a guest were cordially invited to a dinner party at their home that evening. Judging from the little cable car shindig Graham had thrown at the Cliff House, this little dinner party was going to be of the ultra swanky variety and she wanted to make sure she could swank right along with the best of them.

Simon had dutifully waited in the other room while she had her measurements taken, retaken, clucked about and jotted down. He sat patiently during her endless dress fittings. He played the perfect boyfriend while she looked for the perfect accessories. Sadly, when it came to jewelry she was way, way out of her depth.

Magritte's Jewelers served only the poshiest of the posh. She'd never owned anything real and even her fakes were bad fakes. Not that she would have bought a lot of jewelry even if she'd had the money. But, as she looked down at a case full of sparkly things, one or two sparkles wouldn't have killed her.

Most of the jewelry was overly ornate, just like nearly everything else in Victorian and Edwardian America. If they could embellish it they did and then they did it again. Still, some of the jewelry was gorgeous. The rings with yellow or rose-gold with a big, but not Texas big, diamond were beautiful. There was one with a simple setting that whispered her name.

"Elizabeth?"

She jumped at the voice.

"See anything you like?" Simon asked at her side.

Her eyes lingered on the solitaire and she felt suddenly silly and embarrassed. None of this was for her. "It's fun to look, but I'm sure Mrs. Eldridge has something I can borrow. I'm not the diamonds type anyway."

Simon looked like he was going to argue the point and part of her wished he would, but he just nodded and asked her where else she needed to go.

Their shopping trip took the better part of the day. When they'd finally finished, the carriage was filled with huge boxes. Plastic bags hadn't appeared on the scene and so every purchase was wrapped carefully and placed in a ridiculously large box and tied up with string. It was like being inside Santa's bag.

Shopping wasn't the only thing that took forever. Getting ready for an elegant dinner was hard work. Her hair was being argumentative and it took over an hour to show it just who was boss.

Little Jane had tried to convince her that face enamel was the makeup for any lady of the day, but Mrs. Eldridge had, thankfully, put the kibosh on that. A little eye pencil, rouge and lip-rouge would be more than enough.

After half an hour of piling on layer after torturous layer of undergarments Elizabeth was ready for her dress. It was even more frightening than the prospect of enameling her face, whatever that was. The dress was probably the most beautiful thing she'd ever seen and she was sure she was going to look like a fool in it.

It was gold satin-velvet with lace insets and velvet appliques. The bodice was golden draped chiffon with a sweetheart neckline. Elizabeth picked up the train she knew she would eventually trip over and looked in the mirror. She'd felt like an idiot when Jane had helped her on with it, but now seeing herself, it was like her fairy godmother had bopped her on the head. A beautiful, if not completely confident woman, stared back at her.

She put on the gold filigree and pearl necklace and matching earrings Mrs. Eldridge loaned her and was ready to make her grand entrance. She stood at the top of the stairs to catch her breath, but the way Simon looked wasn't helping. Confident, dapper and seriously *en fuego*. She'd always thought tails were kind of silly, but on Simon silly wasn't the word that came to mind. "Hot damn" summed it up nicely.

She put a hand on the banister and started down the stairs. In the movies, the heroine always glided down the stairs so gracefully. Props to them, because it wasn't easy. Effortless grace took a lot of work. She tried to keep her eyes on Simon, but she nearly missed a step and tightened her death grip on the banister. Effortless was definitely out of reach. At this point, she'd happily settle for not going ass over teakettle.

"So beautiful," Simon said as he took her hand and helped her down the last few steps.

"It is, isn't it?" Elizabeth said smoothing down the silk skirt.

"I wasn't talking about the dress, Elizabeth."

No matter how often he complimented her, it still caught her off guard.

Simon leaned in close. "How important is it that we're on time?" He kissed her cheek and then her neck. "Would they miss us if we were an hour or two late?"

She managed not to lose all of her focus. "That might be pushing it."

He nibbled on the nape of her neck. "Twenty minutes?"

"You're a very bad man."

"I'm trying to be."

The carriage ride to the Graham's took all of two minutes which was a good thing considering they were running fifteen minutes late. They lived just a few blocks over on the knob of Nob Hill. She'd thought Mrs. Eldridge house was big, but the Graham's was Big Four big. This was the sort of place she expected a robber baron like Crocker to live in. Maybe Mary's father had been one of the railroad kings.

The mansion was enormous and a little frightening. Maybe it was the foggy San Francisco evening, but it looked spooky, like Disneyland's Haunted Mansion on steroids or the truly disturbing Winchester House in San Jose. Her nerves were definitely starting to get the better of her. She really needed to stop watching the Discovery Channel.

They were ushered into a large foyer where several servants helped them with their hats and coats. The butler then led them to a huge set of double doors.

"Your names, sir?"

"Sir Simon Cross and Miss Elizabeth West."

Simon was completely at ease, but she felt a little like Julia Roberts out on a date with Richard Gere. She tried not to fidget and swallowed a nervous laugh. Simon held out his arm and whispered reassurances in her ear.

"Right. Courage, Camille." She picked up her train and took his arm when she realized that she'd completely forgotten to ask him about his sudden title. "Sir Simon?"

He shrugged. "Just a minor baronetcy."

Amazing. She wasn't even sure what a baronetcy was, but she was pretty sure there was nothing minor about it. How could he be so nonchalant about it all? "And I suppose you have a castle too."

"No."

"Good."

"There is a family estate, but—"

The butler opened one of the doors and stood back. "Sir Simon Cross and Miss Elizabeth West."

They entered the large, lavish parlor. The entire room was paneled in a rich, deep mahogany and candled chandeliers gave off a warm yellow glow. A string quartet played something classical from their spot on the far side of the room. Victor Graham, looking smart and very at home in his tuxedo, excused himself from a small group of his other guests and greeted them. Elizabeth introduced Simon, stumbling over his title.

About a dozen guests dressed to the nines, tens and elevens, enjoyed cocktails and chatted. All of them greeted her with what seemed to be genuine smiles and compliments. Simon was quickly pulled away to explain what it was like to be a baronet. She'd love to hear that herself. She was herded into a circle of ladies talking about the upcoming opera. Simon had tried to introduce her to opera. She'd fallen asleep in their box. She was more Pal Joey than Puccini.

She smiled, nodded and small talked with the ladies at the party. But no matter how hard she tried, she still felt like a stranger in a very strange land until she heard a friendly voice.

"Peanut?"

CHAPTER FIFTEEN

"TEDDY!" ELIZABETH BLURTED OUT a bit too loudly. She was so relieved to see a familiar face; she'd let a little too much Texas out. "I didn't expect to see you here. I didn't realize you were close to the Grahams."

Teddy tucked his little brown sack of peanuts into his jacket pocket and brushed a straggler off his lapel. "I'm not."

"But you were at the other party and this looks pretty exclusive."

"Oh, it is!" he said with a bright smile. "I wouldn't be here if I weren't rich though."

Elizabeth couldn't help but laugh. Teddy's unfiltered honesty was so refreshing. "Graham hitting you up for an investment?"

Teddy nodded. "But you're here because you're wonderful."

"I wouldn't go that far."

He ducked his head. "I would."

"Would what?" Simon said appearing at their side.

Like a rabbit seeing a hunter, Teddy fidgeted in place for a second and then tried to make a quick escape. Elizabeth grabbed his arm. "Teddy, I'd like you to meet, Simon—Sir Simon Cross. Simon, this is Teddy Fiske."

Simon stuck out his hand. "Fiske."

Without looking up, Teddy's head bobbed and shook Simon's hand with one quick pump. "Hi."

"Teddy's the one I was telling you about. He has a photographic memory."

"Eidetic," Teddy said. "From the Greek *eidos*, something seen. It's not technically photographic."

She'd warned Simon about Teddy's eccentricity, but Teddy was something that had to experience firsthand to be fully understood. She prayed Simon did.

"I stand corrected," Simon said politely.

Teddy frowned. "I'm sorry. Sometimes I'm rude and I don't mean to be. You look beautiful."

Elizabeth laughed. "That's all right, Teddy. Some of my favorite people do that," she said as she glanced up at Simon. "And thank you."

"Sorry to interrupt," Victor Graham said as he joined them by the fireplace. "You gentlemen don't mind if I steal my tomato girl?"

Both men nodded, but clearly neither was happy with the prospect of being left with the other. As she was pulled away, Elizabeth gave Simon a pleading look with emphasis on Teddy, who looked like a child left on the school steps for his first day of kindergarten.

Simon arched an eyebrow, but turned back to Fiske. "So, I understand you worked with Tesla."

The dinner itself was served in a large formal dining room. There was a big, not quite Citizen Kane big, fireplace where the flames from the fire cast eerie shadows on the opposite wall. An ornate crystal chandelier with dozens of cream-colored candles hovered over the beautifully laid table. A tapestry of a traditional

English hunt covered the wall behind the head of the table and a large mirror the opposite. Simon was seated across the table from her, which made conversation nearly impossible. Thank heaven Teddy was sitting next to her.

The table setting was ridiculously complex. Elizabeth could feel the sweat forming in her palms. The most formal dinner she'd attended was at Mexican Pete's daughter's *quinceanera*. And that was ten years ago and in a VWF hall. Of course, Simon had taken her to some very nice restaurants, but it was always just the two of them. If she used her fish fork to eat her salad, only Simon knew. She glanced down at the place setting in front of her—four forks, three spoons, two knives and a disaster waiting to happen.

She was careful to watch the other guests before she made any moves. In the end, it wasn't difficult to follow along, but pacing herself was. Eight courses was five or six too many.

And then there was the booze—cocktails beforehand, sherry with the first courses, then several glasses of wine or champagne and finally port or Madeira. Luckily, she'd barely sipped each glass. For all the repressed trappings of Victorian society, they partied hearty.

Somewhere between the soup and the fish, Victor Graham had offered a toast to his rescuer. The group drank to her health and laughed as Graham recounted their adventure. Unfortunately, Elizabeth's x-gene of invisibility still hadn't manifested itself and so all she could do was smile and suffer gracefully.

Graham was much as he had been at the Cliff House—amiable, talkative and entertaining. Mary Graham, on the other hand, sat quietly at the other end of the table doing more rearranging of her food than eating it. Even in the yellow glow of the candles and lamplight, she looked pale. She smiled politely and made small talk with the couple seated at her end of the table, but she was a far cry from the convivial host her husband was.

Over three hours later, when the last course had been cleared, the men retired to a smoking room for cigars and brandy and the ladies to the salon for a demitasse or a cordial. After all that food, all Elizabeth wanted was some Alka-Seltzer and a six or seven hour nap.

Mary Graham remained pinched in the face and waved off any offers of drink. She joined in the conversations and was actually quite bright. Elizabeth expected the talk to be all frippery and fashion, but the ladies surprised her. They talked about politics, philosophy and art and even listened in earnest to Elizabeth when she had something to offer. It was nearly midnight when Victor Graham opened the doors to the ladies' salon and announced that the night's entertainment was about to begin. The room was instantly abuzz with anticipation.

Elizabeth found Simon in the hall. "It's a marathon, isn't it?" '

"And too much for some," he said gesturing to the smoking room where Teddy was fast asleep in an overstuffed leather chair. "We lost him about an hour ago."

He looked adorable as he hugged a pillow to his chest. "Poor Teddy."

"We'll make sure he gets home after the…entertainment. God help us."

The party, which had shed a few members and was down to eight, was escorted into yet another salon. All the occasional chairs and tables had been pushed against the walls or removed and were replaced by a large oval table. It was draped with a heavy red velvet tablecloth and ringed with nine hardback chairs.

At the center of the table amidst a cluster of candles sat a lidless tureen of soup and a basket of bread. The overly sweet scent of incense filled the room and the wisps of smoke disappeared up into the dark of the ceiling.

"Welcome to our séance," Graham said with a wicked smile. Mary Graham stood at his side and seemed far less enthused at the idea.

A figure stepped out of the shadows. "Please be seated."

"Petrovka," Simon whispered in Elizabeth's ear as he held out her chair.

So this was the mysterious Madame Petrovka. Simon had described her well. She was a far cry from the gypsy fortunetellers and new age mystics she'd seen back home. Madame Petrovka was definitely different.

Madame Petrovka gestured to a small, wiry man who followed her out of the shadows. "My assistant, Mr. Stryker, will join us to make the circle complete."

Slugworth had nothing on Mr. Stryker. As if he wasn't scary enough, he had a long scar that ran from the corner of his mouth down to his chin. It made him look a little like a ventriloquist's dummy. And those turned up the creepy dial to eleven. Elizabeth nudged Simon and gestured questioningly toward Stryker. Simon shrugged in response.

"Now, it is vitally important," Mrs. Petrovka said slowly, "that everyone here be open to the idea of the Other World. The spirits will not come to us if they sense negative energy. I must ask that if you cannot give yourself completely that you leave the circle now."

No one moved to leave. Simon even managed to keep a straight face. She knew how he felt about these things. Despite having seen proof that the paranormal was more than fiction, he was still a skeptic. Elizabeth wasn't exactly Mulder to his Scully, but she knew that the truth lay somewhere between them.

Elizabeth had never been to a real séance before. The closest she'd come was playing Light As a Feather, Stiff As a Board with some other kids at a local motel just outside of El Paso. Chanting and lifting a sixty pound seven year old off the floor with "just their wills" and a few fingers didn't seem as impressive now as it had then. She had the feeling this séance would probably be a little more involved than that.

"Very good." Madame Petrovka took her seat at the head of the table with Stryker to her left and Mary Graham to her right. "You are clearing your minds now. Please close your eyes. Breathe deeply. All together, please?"

Everyone took a few deep breaths. The smoke from the incense was so thick Elizabeth could taste it. It was sweet, earthy and floral.

"You are relaxing and opening to the world around you," Madame Petrovka said. Her voice was breathy and yet, compelling, even commanding. "We want the spirits of the Other World to know that we welcome them. We are open to them and we hope they will join us. Please open your eyes and take the hands of the persons sitting next to you."

Simon took hold of Elizabeth's right hand and squeezed it. Victor Graham held her left. Madame Petrovka nodded and Mr. Stryker blew out all but three candles.

"Good, you are still relaxed and open. You must not let go of each other's hands. The circle must not be broken. We make an offering of food to the spirits to nurture them and we invite them to join us."

This lady was good. Elizabeth hadn't felt so good and relaxed in ages. All of the tension from the dinner had faded away and everything seemed wonderful.

"I will now try to summon any spirits that are amongst us. You must not break the circle no matter what may occur. We are all safe and open to the Other World."

Madame Petrovka's eyes fluttered closed and she dipped her head. "Our beloved spirits, we bring you gifts from life unto death. Commune with us and move among us. If you are here, give us a sign."

A long silence followed where all Elizabeth could hear was her own heartbeat.

"We welcome, beloved spirit. Come among us. We reach out to you. Give us a sign."

A sudden and loud rapping sound from the middle of the table sent a collective gasp through the room.

"We are so pleased you've come to us," Madame Petrovka said. "You are welcome among us, spirit. Do you want to speak to us?"

Another loud knock came.

"Are you familiar with this place?

Another, a little louder than before.

"Can you tell us who you are?"

There was another long pause and then small flowers fluttered down from the ceiling. Violets. Victor Graham's hand spasmed around hers.

Mary Graham cried out.

"Do not break the circle!"

"This means something to you?" Madame Petrovka prompted.

Mary Graham was softly crying and couldn't speak. Her husband cleared his throat. "Our… our daughter's name was Violet."

"She has passed on?"

"Two years ago," Graham said softly.

"Beloved spirit," Madame Petrovka said, "are you Violet Graham?"

There was a long silent pause before a loud, sure knock made Mrs. Graham let out another strangled cry.

"We should stop this," Victor said, but Mary cut him off.

"No, please."

Madame Petrovka nodded and closed her eyes. "Violet, you are welcome here. Your parents miss you very much. Would you like to talk to them?"

The rapping on the table came again.

"Yes, I sense her now."

"Violet," Mary said through her tears. "We miss you so much, darling."

Elizabeth was fascinated, but felt like an intruder at the same time. Real or not, this was deeply personal.

"She loved you very much," Madame Petrovka said. "She… something's wrong. What's wrong, Violet?"

"What is it?" Graham asked.

"She's frightened."

"It's all right, darling," Mary said.

"She's moving," Madame Petrovka said. "Why are you running, child? Are you playing a game?"

The chandelier crystals clinked as it shook. A glass clattered against a tray on the far side of the room. A chair moved as it if had been bumped and suddenly Elizabeth felt something ice cold pass through her. She must have gasped because Simon clenched her hand in his and was looking at her with concern.

"I felt her," Mary cried. "She passed right through me!"

"She seems upset," Madame Petrovka said. "How did she die?"

Graham answered in a hushed and hoarse voice. "Drowned. She was just four."

"Sometimes spirits, especially the young, don't understand what's happened to them," Madame Petrovka said. "Are you afraid to cross over, child?"

She appeared to be listening to a voice only she heard. "What's wrong, child?"

She listened again and her face grew grim. "Everyone must remain calm no matter what should happen next."

"What's going on?" Graham demanded.

"She is not alone."

"What do you mean not alone?" Graham said getting more agitated with every passing second.

"There is a presence with her."

"We're here, darling. Don't be afraid," Mary said.

"It is whispering to her, always in the shadows." Abruptly, Madame Petrovka's demeanor changed. She was stern and angry. "Get away from the other, Violet. Right now!"

"What's happening to her?" Mary cried as she looked desperately from Madame Petrovka to her husband.

"Tell her to do as I say!"

"Listen to her, Violet," Mary said, looking around the room trying in vain to see her child in the darkness. "Do what she says. Move away."

"It's looking for her. It's…" Madame Petrovka's head fell to her chest. Slowly, she raised her head again and when she opened her eyes they were black. She opened her mouth and a sound Elizabeth would never forget came out. It was low and rasping and horrible. It grew louder and louder until it filled the room. Mary Graham screamed.

Elizabeth gripped Simon's hand more tightly. Mr. Stryker lurched from his seat and grabbed Madame Petrovka by the shoulders and yelled into her face, "Be gone!"

Simon jumped out of his chair and stood behind Elizabeth's chair, his hands resting protectively on her shoulders. The sound was horrible.

It reached a crescendo with a thunderous clap and the sound stopped. Madame Petrovka blinked and seemed to come back to herself. Mary Graham cried and Victor tried to comfort her. The rest of the room sat in stunned silence as a wind blew through the windowless room and snuffed out the candles leaving them in pitch black.

Chapter Sixteen

SIMON THREW OPEN THE doors to the hall and called for the servants. He cursed under his breath knowing he should have stopped this charade sooner. A maid and footman hurried inside. The man lit the gas lamps and the room glowed back to life.

Elizabeth went to Mary Graham who was near hysteria. She tried to comfort her, but the woman was barely listening. The other couples dithered about unsure and frightened.

Victor tried his best to calm his wife, but it was no use. "Ellen," he barked to the maid. "Take Mrs. Graham to her room."

The young girl nodded and took a step toward her mistress. She stopped and looked down at the carpet. There were small wet footprints leading to Mrs. Graham's chair. "Sir?"

"Take her," Victor said, easing his wife out of her chair and into the maid's arms.

Madame Petrovka had left the table and stood on the edge of the room, appearing faint and breathing heavily. Mr. Stryker held her arm and whispered in her ear. She nodded. "I'm sorry, Mr. Graham. I must recover."

She started to leave, but Graham blocked her path. "What was that? What are you playing at?"

Madame Petrovka looked at him sadly. Mr. Stryker strode forward and tried to move Graham out of the way. "Later. She needs rest."

Graham was clearly torn, but stepped aside and let them leave. The rest of the party fled the room leaving Simon and Elizabeth alone with Graham and leaving them all wondering what in the hell had just happened.

Graham's breath was still ragged and his eyes were a little wild. Simon didn't blame him in the least. He gave Graham a moment and the man composed himself as best he could. "I apologize. This was not the entertainment I had in mind."

Simon knelt near one of the small footprints on the rug and felt the wetness. "Water." He smelled it and then brought a finger to his mouth and tasted it. "Salt water."

Graham looked like he'd been hit in the stomach. "Sea water." His face paled again and he struggled not to break down. "Please excuse me," he said and fled the room.

Elizabeth looked at Simon anxiously. "What the hell was that, Simon?"

"I don't know." He picked up an oil lamp from the credenza and lit the wick. "But I plan to find out."

He knelt again and studied the small footprints, even lifting up the edge of the rug. He walked the perimeter of the room carefully scanning for wires, tubes, any sort of tampering. They searched under the table and above the chandelier. Nothing looked to be out of place, no hidden mechanisms or any of the usual tricks of the trade.

Confident he'd searched as best he could, he turned to Elizabeth. That's when he noticed how pale she was and that she was actually shivering. He took off his dinner jacket and slipped it over her shoulders. "Let's go home."

Elizabeth gave the violets that covered the tabletop one last glance and then nodded. They gathered up Teddy who was still sleeping soundly in the other room. After helping him out to his carriage, they got into their own and started back to Mrs. Eldridge's.

"Are you all right?" Simon asked.

"I'm fine. I just…you didn't feel it?"

Simon rubbed one of her hands between his. It was ice cold. "Feel what?"

Elizabeth shivered. "I don't know. It felt like jumping into ice water."

"Can you remember anything else?"

"I don't know. It was right before that…what was that, Simon?"

He didn't answer. As much as he'd love to believe they'd witnessed an actual paranormal event, he knew that everything they'd seen that night could be explained. Somehow. Given enough time, he'd figure out Madame Petrovka's tricks. Regardless, whatever had happened the effects on the Grahams and Elizabeth were real enough.

"I don't know what it was," Elizabeth said sounding much more like her old self, "But I'm not a fan."

When they arrived back at Mrs. Eldridge's, Gerald greeted them at the door. "Good eve—What's wrong?" he asked Elizabeth. "What happened?" he demanded of Simon.

"Tea, lots of it," Simon said.

"English," Gerald muttered, but he left to start the tea.

Simon and Elizabeth went into the front parlor. She was still shivering and Simon pulled a chair in front of the hearth. He stoked the fire and lit a few lamps. "Better?"

"That was genuinely disturbing, Simon."

He pulled a chair close to hers. "Yes, it was," he said with a deep frown. "And a little too coincidental, don't you think? The man you're sent here to save is the victim of a charlatan days before his murder?"

Though Elizabeth nodded, he could see the doubt in her eyes. "That was more than smoke and mirrors though, Simon. And, besides, what could she gain from that?"

"Control? Blackmail? I don't know. But I do know that what happened was not what it appeared to be."

Elizabeth shook her head. "Color me unconvinced. You searched the room. How do you explain the flowers? And that thing at the end."

"There's an explanation."

"What if it was real?"

Simon didn't have an answer to that. "I believe that we should consider the possible before the impossible."

"You didn't—" Elizabeth started, but Gerald entered with a tray of tea. He set it down on the table and stood looking down at Simon with a disapproving frown.

"Yes?" Simon said tartly. He didn't know why, but Gerald did not like him.

"You should know better than take a lady like her to places like that."

"What on earth are you on about?" Simon asked.

"Chinatown at this time of night and those places—"

"Chinatown? We went to the Graham's," Elizabeth said.

"What makes you think we went to Chinatown?" Simon asked.

"Your clothes," Gerald said. "I know that smell. Opium. That's not for the likes of you, girl."

"Opium?" Simon said.

"We didn't—"

"The incense." Simon shook his head silently berating himself for not having realized it sooner. "It was laced with opium. Would a real medium need to drug her audience?"

"No," Elizabeth admitted. "You're sure that's what it is, Gerald."

"It's a not smell you forget."

"Thank you," Simon said, dismissing him.

Gerald completely ignored him and looked to Elizabeth who said, "I'm okay. He's not so bad when you get to know him."

Gerald didn't look like he agreed, but he bowed and left them alone. The man was irritating, although Simon knew he should be grateful that he had Elizabeth's best interest at heart.

Simon poured the tea and handed Elizabeth a cup. She held it in both hands and stared into it. "Opium's addictive, isn't it? What if I'm an addict now and sell everything I own for my next fix?"

Simon chuckled. "I wouldn't worry. I doubt we ingested enough smoke for that. Just enough for us to be pretty little marks."

Elizabeth sipped her tea. "Whatever that was at the end, Simon, her eyes and that sound…" She shivered again at the memory.

"It was impressive."

"Creepy as hell."

Simon conceded that point. "But remember, we were plied with food and drink for hours. We were tired and, not to mention, apparently drugged. All of that made us infinitely more susceptible to suggestion. The success of the deception depends on that. The mood, the manipulation, the willingness to suspend common sense. You know from our research that nearly every inexplicable event is eventually explained."

"*Nearly* every one."

Simon couldn't argue with that, but it didn't change how he felt. He put his teacup down and gazed into the fire.

"I think the real question we should be asking isn't how she did it, but why? If our Madame Petrovka isn't what she appears to be, what does she want from Graham and, more importantly, how far will she go to get it?"

The next morning, Simon found himself back where he'd started, waiting impatiently. He looked around the parlor for something to occupy himself while Elizabeth dressed. If she felt the same way he did, it might take her some time. He wished she'd let him stay with her. It would have been so much easier if they'd simply give up the pretense and share rooms. But Elizabeth didn't want to offend Mrs. Eldridge and so he'd gone back to his hotel last night and suffered a fitful night's sleep.

It had been less than eight hours since he'd seen her and yet, he missed her. It probably wasn't healthy, but then he was still new to the feeling. New to wanting to be with someone, of wanting to be home. After all, he'd spent most of his life wishing he were anywhere else. And his parents were more than happy to oblige.

As with most boys in his position, he'd been shipped off to boarding school at the first opportunity. Eton was only marginally better than the cold and foreboding Grey Hall. At school his reclusive nature had been honed by a creative cruelty reserved for the entitled English schoolboy. He'd become one of them before long, learning to cut without drawing blood. It was a skill that had served him well through the years and one that had kept him always on the outside looking in.

It was only the summers in Sussex with his grandfather that had saved him. Those few months had somehow planted the seeds of a good man inside the fallow schoolboy he'd been. He hadn't done much of anything to nurture them. Despite his neglect, they'd somehow managed to take root. What else could explain a woman like Elizabeth being in his life?

Simon reached for the tea the maid Jane had brought him, but it had gone cold. Pushing it away, he rose from the settee and walked over to the fireplace. He stared up at the portrait of Evan Eldridge. The old man's face reminded him a bit of his grandfather. They didn't really look anything alike, but there was a spark in the eyes, an understanding and a kindness that Simon envied. Would he ever look in the mirror and see that expression looking back?

"He was a wonderful man," Mrs. Eldridge said at his shoulder.

He'd been so caught up in his thoughts he hadn't heard her come in. "I'm sorry. Yes, I'm sure he was." Simon cleared his throat and turned his back on the portrait, suddenly uncomfortable. "Is Elizabeth ready yet?"

"Waiting's terribly difficult, isn't it?" Mrs. Eldridge said before returning her gaze to her husband. "If you are not too long, I will wait here for you all of my life." She turned back to Simon with a wan smile. "If only my heart knew what too long was."

Simon clasped his hands behind his back. "The heart has its reasons for which reason knows nothing of."

"Pascal? Just so." Mrs. Eldridge gestured for Simon to have a seat. He hesitated, but sat back down on the settee. "If you don't mind an old woman's meddling—"

"Please, you're not—"

"Old or meddling? I'm both, I'm afraid. But, if you'll indulge me..."

Simon wanted to stop her. He was uncomfortable with conversations like this under the best of circumstances and according to Elizabeth Mrs. Eldridge had a way of seeing right to a person's heart. He didn't protest though; he merely inclined his head politely.

Mrs. Eldridge folded her hands in her lap. "Trust her."

Simon waited for the rest of it. Surely, there was more to it than that. He was a little confused when she didn't follow up with more. "Yes, thank you. I do."

She laughed lightly. "It sounds so simple, doesn't it? But trust doesn't come easily for some and too easily for others. I suspect you're the former and she's the latter."

Simon nodded. Truer words were never spoken. It was a trait in Elizabeth that he found both maddening and endearing.

"More tea?"

"No, thank you."

"My mother always felt everything was better with tea. I was never so inclined," she admitted.

"Your one flaw," Simon teased.

Mrs. Eldridge smiled and then grew serious again. "I have many I assure you. There was a time when I was terribly selfish."

Simon started to protest, but her raised hand silenced him. "No, it's quite true. You see, I thought I could wait, patiently, for Evan to return from whatever mysterious adventure he was on. Usually, he returned almost at the same moment he'd left. But there were times when he was gone for weeks, months. And the lie I'd told myself started to sour my otherwise sweet and charming personality," she said with a self-deprecating smile.

"Until finally, I asked Evan to stop. I begged him to destroy the watch and stay with me. I told him that if he loved me, he'd do as I asked. Much to my shame, he did. He knew what love was better than I and it took some time for me to realize what I'd done."

She stood and walked back to the portrait. Simon reflexively stood in response. "He didn't resent me," she said turning back to Simon. "He was too fine a man for that. But I'd destroyed something in him. Some crucial part of him. Something that made him the man I loved in the first place.

"Those were very dark times," she said clasping her hands tightly in front of her. "Love tests us in many ways, Mr. Cross. And each requires a unique kind of courage. Trusting someone, allowing them beyond our grasp, can be the most difficult of all."

That particular truth was razor sharp and Simon knew the pain of its cut all too well.

The door to the salon opened and Elizabeth breezed in, pinning her hat as she walked. "Simon, I was—" she said and stopped as she noticed he wasn't alone. "Oh, Good morning, Mrs. Eldridge."

"Good morning, dear," Mrs. Eldridge said. She met Elizabeth at the door and fixed an errant curl in Elizabeth's hair. "There. Now, have a good day and try not to get into too much trouble."

She glanced back at Simon and smiled at him under her pince-nez. "Some of us are rather fond of you."

Elizabeth had a headache that wouldn't quit. That morning when she'd asked Jane if they had something she could take the little maid's face had lit up. She'd brought Elizabeth a basket of assorted pills, powders and tonics. The girl was apparently more than a bit of a hypochondriac.

There were nerve and brain pills, blood pills, liver pills and the always disturbing worm cakes. She took a pass on Dr. Rose's French Arsenic wafers and Sears Roebuck's Egyptian Pile Cure. Finally, she'd found a bottle of aspirin powder. Happily, it had done the trick.

Bless you, Bayer.

She was sure that without it her brains would have been shriveled enough that they would have bounced right out of her head. The carriage hit another pothole and Elizabeth's stomach lurched in protest.

"I hope it isn't too early to call," she said as they arrived at the Graham's.

"I don't think so," Simon said. "It's nearly noon."

They were asked to wait in a small front parlor which was clearly designed for short, here's your hat what's your hurry visits.

A few minutes later Mary Graham joined them. She looked much better than she had last night, but was still pallid and nervous. She offered her husband's apologies. He was feeling a little under the weather this morning.

"I don't mean to pry, Mrs. Graham," Simon said, "how did you find Madame Petrovka?"

"Victor suggested we have a séance. I don't know how he found her. I've never been quite sure how I feel about those things, but he thought it would be… entertaining."

The sadness in her eyes nearly broke Elizabeth's heart.

"I know how you must feel," Simon said.

Mary Graham regarded him with surprisingly steely gray eyes. "Do you have any children, Sir Simon?"

"No."

"Then I don't think you do know how I feel."

"No," Simon said clearing his throat uncomfortably. "You're quite right. I can only imagine it. I do know, however, that if someone used my child like that, nothing on heaven or earth would stop me from finding out why."

"Used her? What do you mean?"

Simon frowned and Elizabeth braced herself for the emotional tidal wave that was sure to follow.

"I believe," Simon said, "that Madame Petrovka is not what she appears to be. As I'm sure you're aware, many of these so-called spiritualists are no more than con artists."

Mary fidgeted in her seat. "Yes, I've heard that, but—"

"They use someone's grief to manipulate them," Simon said.

Mary looked near the verge of tears. Elizabeth laid a hand on Simon's forearm to stop him. Mary wasn't ready for this kind of conversation. An uncomfortable silence began.

Elizabeth saw a picture of a young girl on one of the end tables and picked it up. "Is this Violet?"

Mary nodded and dabbed her eyes.

The girl in the photograph looked about four years old. She was a beautiful little thing in a light summer dress squatting down over a tide pool.

"She loved that spot," Mary said gesturing to the photograph.

Elizabeth handed Simon the photograph and turned back to Mary. "What happened?"

Fighting back the tears, Mary nodded. She started to speak, but faltered. The pain in the woman's eyes was like a living thing. "If it's too difficult…"

"She and Victor were off on one of their outings. They used to go off together and have little adventures. They both loved the ocean. I was never too fond of it, so I stayed home."

She paused and Elizabeth could feel her summon the courage to continue. "They went down by the rocks, not far from where that photograph was taken, near Land's End. He turned his back less than a minute and…she'd crawled out and he'd…he'd told her so many times not to do that…and a wave must have come and taken…taken her."

The tears were coming freely now. "It was an accident, a horrible accident, but he blames himself. I don't think a day goes by that he doesn't torture himself about what happened that day."

Elizabeth had no idea what to say. "I can't imagine how you must be feeling after last night."

Mary dabbed the corners of her eyes with a kerchief. "It's harder on Victor, I think."

"If this was a cruel trick, can you think of anyone who'd want to hurt you or your husband?" Simon asked.

Mary shook her head. "No, not like this." She pulled at the lace trim of her sleeve. "What if that really was our Violet? Reaching out to us?"

"Then we'll find a way to help her," Elizabeth said. "I promise." It was an absurd promise, but she couldn't help herself. She didn't dare look at Simon. She could just imagine the look on his face.

Mary covered her mouth with her kerchief and grimaced. She took a spoonful of tonic from a tray on the side table. "You'll forgive me," she said as she stood. "It seems I'm not feeling all that well myself."

Simon stood and helped her to the door. "Thank you for seeing us."

"Henry will see you out."

Out front of the Graham's, the coachman opened the door to their carriage for them.

Simon reached out to help her into the carriage, but Elizabeth shook her head. "Let's walk. I could use the air."

Simon nodded to the coachman sending him on his way and then wound Elizabeth's arm through his.

They started back to Mrs. Eldridge's. "That was quite a promise," he said.

"I know it's crazy. I just kept thinking how I'd feel if it was our daughter."

She cast a quick glance at Simon, but his expression was unreadable. They'd never discussed children. They'd never even discussed pets. Heck, they weren't even engaged. But she did wonder though, more often than she'd like to admit, if he even wanted a family. His previous family experience had pretty much stunk on ice. Not that she wanted kids. Not right now anyway, but someday. Maybe.

"If it had been our daughter, neither one of them would have left that room under their own power."

Elizabeth's stomach flipped at the fierceness in his voice. It was probably wrong to feel this way, she thought, but that was damn sexy.

He ground his teeth and then continued, "Regardless, we need to know more about Madame Petrovka. All we know so far is that she lived in England for several years."

"Max has some friends there. Maybe he could cable them, ask them to poke around?"

"Good. And speaking of Mr. Harrington."

Elizabeth raised a hand to stop him. "I know. I'll talk to him today. I can just see it. 'So sorry, Max, I'm not interested, by the way would you like to do me a favor?' Smooth."

"It's better than pistols at dawn."

Elizabeth laughed although the image of Simon dueling wasn't actually hard to conjure. "I'll talk to him."

"We should also find out what we can about those union workers."

"And the Admiral," Elizabeth said. "Although, he doesn't seem the sort."

"Men have done far more for far less," Simon reminded her.

That was true enough and far from comforting. The weight of it all was starting to feel a little overwhelming. "I wish we had more time. Even if we do discover who wants him dead I don't know how we're going to stop it."

"We'll find a way," Simon said, pulling her closer. "It's what we do."

Chapter Seventeen

Max was very understanding. Too understanding. She'd told him that she and Simon had been together in New York, had fought and were now trying to make it work. It wasn't a lie really and she thought she told it fairly well, but Maxwell just smiled and nodded. And he'd seemed more than happy to help when she'd asked him to look into Madame Petrovka. He didn't even ask any questions about why she wanted to know. He just grinned that trillion-watt smile of his and promised to do his best. It was unnerving. Either she was becoming as suspicious as Simon or she wasn't actually all that and a bag of Skittles.

While she'd been letting Max down easily, Simon had been looking for the Union Labor Party headquarters. During the time he'd been looking for her, he'd cultivated his minor army of spies, who for a few coins would be happy to tell him just about anything about anyone.

He learned that the man Elizabeth had intercepted that day at the Ferry Building was named Olaf Karlsson. Judging from the anger Olaf and his comrades had shown at Graham during his speech, they were definitely potential problems. Olaf and a few others were making a speech at Lotta's Fountain near the Palace Hotel.

By the time Elizabeth and Simon arrived a small crowd was already gathering.

"Over there," Elizabeth said, pointing toward Olaf and the heckler from the speech who were leaning against the fountain watching the crowd.

She and Simon made their way to the two men. "Mr. Karlsson."

"You!" Olaf said shoving himself away from the fountain.

Simon stepped forward and raised a hand. "We're just here to talk."

"Len does all of our talking," Olaf said jerking a thumb toward the other man.

The little man smiled revealing rows of crooked, yellowing teeth. "And boy am I gonna do some talking today."

"You should go," Olaf said to Elizabeth.

"I'm sorry about what happened. I thought you were going shoot him or something."

"Or something," Len said stepping out into the street.

"I really am sorry, but there have been threats made to Mr. Graham and you and your—"

"This is no place for you," Olaf said.

She was definitely getting a little tired of people telling her that. Simon, Gerald, and now Olaf. Why did every man in creation think they were suddenly the boss of her?

That's when she heard it. First it was just a brass band approaching from the distance and then voices. Lots of them. She and Simon stepped out into the street. Turning the corner of Market and Kearney had to be hundreds of men with a large red banner at the front that said "Workingmen Unite!"

Red banners were never good.

"Aw, crap," Elizabeth mumbled.

"Agreed."

In less than a minute they were surrounded and buffeted about in the crowd. Simon wrapped his arm around Elizabeth and tried to weave his way toward the hotel.

Len was hoisted up onto one of the corners of the fountain. "Like our brother Haywood, we will not be controlled. Put our blood here!"

A few other men climbed the fountain to string up the banner, but a group of blue-coated police appeared and that's when all hell broke loose. The crowd became a mob. Fights broke out indiscriminately all around them. Bricks, iron scrap and slabs of terra cotta from a nearby construction site were instant missiles.

A group of men jumped on a passing cable car and pulled the passengers right out of their seats. Police rushed in, but they were completely overwhelmed. And Simon and Elizabeth found themselves trapped in the middle of a full-scale riot.

Simon held her close to his chest as he tried to hurry them through the crowd, but they were blocked at every turn. Elizabeth was shoved and grabbed. Something akin to genuine panic started to well up inside her when someone jabbed her in the ribs, hard, and she cried out in pain. She heard a loud thud and then iron hands gripped her arm. But they weren't Simon's. She spun her head around to see Olaf, red faced and with a small trickle of blood running down from a cut above his left eye.

"This way," he yelled and then pushed, shoved and tossed people aside. With raw brute force, he cut a path through the crowd. Luckily, the melee started to thin on the sidewalks near the front of the Palace Hotel.

Just as Olaf propelled them toward the front door, a policeman cracked him on the back of the head with a billy club. Olaf's head snapped forward and his legs wobbled. Another officer grabbed him by the arm and started to drag Olaf away.

Elizabeth tried to go to him. "He just was helping us!"

But she couldn't move. Simon held on to her too tightly and dragged her past the doormen into the hotel. The big doors shut behind them and they stumbled into the surreal quiet of the hotel lobby. Everything felt unnatural like it does just after a car accident and she felt the tingle of adrenaline.

"We should help him," Elizabeth said.

Simon shook his head. "It's too late. There's nothing we can do now."

Even though she knew he was right, Elizabeth was ready to argue, but a sharp pain in here side stopped her.

"Are you hurt?" Simon said.

She shook her head, but Simon wasn't convinced. "Come on," he said as he guided her to the bank of elevators, stopping only briefly at the front desk to get his key and bark some orders. "Uncanny," he muttered.

"What?"

"You and trouble."

"It's a gift."

Once they were safely inside his rooms, Simon quickly shed his jacket and set about tending to Elizabeth. She'd taken off her hat and, thankfully, didn't look to be too much worse for the wear.

He helped her off with her jacket and then gently probed her side. "How bad is it? Be honest."

"A little sore, but not bad. Honestly."

He wasn't sure he believed her. She had an unnatural aversion to going to hospital. "Just a flesh wound?"

She smiled and laughed a little. "I'm fine, really."

His fingers deftly moved across her ribs. "I think your corset might have taken the brunt of it."

"Finally good for something."

"You should take it off though."

"Why, Sir Simon!"

He hadn't set out to make this a seduction, but now that he looked at her beautifully flushed face and imagined the prospect of making love to her, it wasn't such a bad idea after all.

"Fine," she said with a resigned sigh. "But it is going to be hell putting that thing back on."

He cupped her cheek and leaned in to whisper in her ear. "Let's just enjoy taking it off, shall we?"

Elizabeth's blush deepened and she started to unbutton her blouse, but he covered her hands with his. He wanted this to last.

"Let me."

A shuddering breath was his answer.

Slowly, he knelt in front of her and unlaced each boot and helped her step out of them. His hands brushed up the back of her stocking legs, inched his way up the garter straps, but stopped mid-thigh. He undid the garter fastenings to her stockings and rolled each down her leg. His fingers brushed against the bare skin of the back of her knee and he heard her gasp. There would be more of that, he thought.

Standing, he gave her a sly smile. "One must do these things properly or not at all."

Her face was even more flushed than before and her beautiful blue eyes were dark with need. "Properly's good."

He smiled again and took off her gloves, kissing the inside of her wrists with just slightest brush of his lips. Her breathy sigh tested his patience, but he wanted to savor this moment.

His fingers started at the notch in her neck and ran down along the buttons of her blouse just between her breasts. She arched her back, straining for his touch, but he wanted her to feel the same need he did. The same burning passion.

He undid the fastenings for her skirt and then with aching slowness began work on the buttons of her blouse from the bottom up. Once he was done, he slipped his warm hands under the fabric, barely grazing her warm soft skin and pushed it back off her shoulders. It fell to the floor and was quickly joined by her thin white cotton corset cover.

She stood before him dressed only in her underclothes now and he nearly lost the last tether on his control. He wanted to have her then. So very badly. The only way quell is aching need was to stop even for the briefest of moments. He leaned closed and blew a feather soft breath on to the nape of her neck. She gasped and rolled her head to the side, hoping to tempt him. God in heaven, he was tempted, but his will was stronger than hers. For now.

Simon walked around behind her, so close he knew she could feel his presence even with eyes closed. His hands brushed across her hips and up over her breasts as he unhooked her corset fastenings from behind. Elizabeth leaned back into his body, her head falling against his shoulder. He put his hands on her waist and pulled her body back against his. He knew then that she could feel his need as keenly as he did.

Her corset fell to the floor forgotten, followed by her bloomers and chemise. She was completely naked now.

His hands barely brushed the swell of her hips as they moved around her. Fingertips grazed her skin as his hands passed over her stomach and up toward her breasts. Finally giving in to his desire, his fingers brushed along the underside of her breasts. He took them into his hands and leaned down to kiss the side of her neck. She arched into touch.

"So beautiful," he whispered.

She eased around in his arms, kissed the corner of his mouth, smiled and then started toward the bedroom leaving him nearly breathless. He watched as she leaned against the doorway, the very picture of the coy seductress. "Are you going to do this properly, or not?"

He unbuttoned his collar and walked toward her. "Definitely not properly."

CHAPTER EIGHTEEN

THICK BLACK SOOT BILLOWED out of the ferry's smokestack and disappeared into the distance behind them. It was a smoother ride than Simon had thought it would be considering how rough the bay could be. Then again, the ferry was no small ship at nearly 300 feet in length and almost half that in width. The coal engine hummed below deck and the side-paddles made an oddly comforting churning sound as they dug through the water.

After Elizabeth and he had recovered from the afternoon's adventures, Simon had used his little spy network again to find the Admiral. It might be a waste of time to talk with him, but waiting for Sunday to come simply wasn't an option.

According to Simon's sources, the Admiral liked to ride the ferries. Supposedly, it reminded him of his navy days and more often than not, he could be found at dusk riding the Bay City ferry to Oakland and back. That's just where Simon and Elizabeth found him, standing at the rail of the cabin deck looking out over the bay.

"Beautiful, isn't it?" Elizabeth said as she joined the Admiral at the railing.

He seemed surprised that anyone had spoken. He turned to her, looked her up and down and then turned back to the sea. "I've always thought so."

"What island is that?" Elizabeth asked.

"Angel Island. It was a fine naval base once. Now, it's home to the devil—coolies and their nursemaids."

Elizabeth turned to Simon and raised an eyebrow. He held up a placating hand. People were products of their world and San Francisco at the turn of the century was not exactly accepting of racial differences.

"Immigration is complicated," Elizabeth said.

The Admiral snorted. "Not from where I stand. Your Graham might call it progress, but to my mind it's the death of a pure America."

Simon could see Elizabeth fighting her instincts to tell the Admiral just what she thought of that last comment. He was proud that she managed to bite out a quick, "I don't work for Graham," instead.

The Admiral snorted. "No? You'll forgive me, Miss, if I have trouble believing that after what I saw the other day."

"That wasn't what it looked like."

"It doesn't really matter. You can tell him I won't fight him anymore. I'm too old and too tired." He turned his attention back to the whitecaps. "At least he can't buy this."

"He really isn't so bad," Elizabeth offered.

The Admiral snorted. "You're just like him, aren't you? Progress at the cost of all else? At the cost of decency? You don't remember how it was before, when the... negros knew their place and the Asiatics stayed where they belonged."

"I thought you fought for the Union."

"I fought for Maryland. The white man doesn't stand a chance now."

"The white man?" Elizabeth said. "The hell?"

The Admiral sighed and looked back out over the water. "I shouldn't expect more than vulgarities from a... woman of your ilk."

"I have an ilk?" Elizabeth narrowed her eyes and cocked her head to the side.

Simon knew this wasn't going to end well and stepped in to intervene. He pulled Elizabeth aside. As much as he wanted to push the damn pillock overboard, he knew he couldn't. "This isn't getting us anywhere, Elizabeth."

"Yes," the Admiral said. "Please control that fishwife."

Simon glared at him, but managed to rein in his impulses. There was nothing to be gained from taking the Admiral apart bigoted piece by bigoted piece, no matter how satisfying it might have felt.

"I think the air's fresher on the other side," Simon said.

He could feel the tension in Elizabeth's body as he led her away. "Makes me crazy," she grumbled. "Miserable old..."

Simon slipped an arm around her waist. "I know, but we can't change him."

They left the Admiral and his hate behind. It had been a disconcerting meeting, made all the more so by knowing that men like him weren't just relics of the past. Even a hundred years later, his brand of hate would still be alive.

The rest of the ferry ride was a rather solemn affair. It was difficult to say whether their encounter with the Admiral had made him less of a suspect or more of one. He was certainly angry enough to be trouble, but Simon didn't get the sense that he was the sort to murder a man in cold blood either. Most men of his type were all talk, but not all of them.

They arrived back at the port just as the sun was dipping below the western horizon. They hired a hack back to Mrs. Eldridge's. Max's car was parked in the flowerbed when they arrived.

While Elizabeth went upstairs to freshen up, Simon went to the salon to wait. Harrington lounged in one of the chairs as he idly flipped through the latest edition of Life Magazine.

"Cross," he said tossing the magazine onto the coffee table. "Where's our darling Elizabeth?"

"My darling Elizabeth is upstairs." Simon eyed the man suspiciously as he sat down opposite him. "I thought she explained our situation."

"Your situation, yes." Harrington picked a piece of fluff off the flower in his lapel button and flicked it away. "It's a funny word for it, isn't it? Situation. Makes it sound so…unsettled."

Simon leaned back and crossed his legs. "Does it?"

Harrington shrugged in that casual, diffident way entitled private schoolboys always did. "If we're being honest with each other. You do prefer that, don't you?"

Simon draped his arms across the back of the small sofa. "By all means."

"Well, then yes, it does sound that way. You and Elizabeth might work things out, but then again, you might not."

"And you'll be there just in case we don't," Simon said feeling less inclined to be polite than he had a few minutes ago.

Harrington shrugged and ran hand through his ridiculously floppy hair. "She's a free woman, has her own mind and I don't see a ring."

Simon was surprised at how calm he was. Just a few days ago a remark like that would have drawn blood, from one of them. "Do you always chase after another man's woman?"

"I'm not chasing, just…running alongside." Harrington laughed. "You probably don't have anything to worry about anyway, old man. Aunt Lillian says I'm not the marrying kind, lack follow-through and all that. Last week I would have said I was in violent agreement with that assessment. I'd be a terrible husband, always setting off on some ridiculous adventure. Of course, if I'd met someone who found the prospect of that as exciting as I do, I'd be a fool to let her go, now wouldn't I?"

Simon was about to respond when Elizabeth came in looking far less sea-blown. "What'd I miss?"

Both men stood and looked at each other. "Nothing."

"All righty then." She sat down next to Simon. "Max, did you find out anything?"

"Quite a bit actually." He walked over to the fireplace and leaned on the mantle. "Your Madame Petrovka has made quite an impression on San Francisco, even before last night's incident."

"How'd you hear about that?" she asked.

"Mrs. Daniels told Mrs. Eckels who told her maid and I lost track after that. I heard it from Teddy who is, by the way, very grateful for your kindness to him last night. Both of you."

Simon nodded his head in acceptance. "And Madame Petrovka?"

"Right. Well, she's predicted things with startling accuracy including the eruption of Mt. Vesuvius."

"That's a pretty big one," Elizabeth said giving Simon a worried look.

"Did you hear back from your contacts in England?" Elizabeth asked.

"One of them. It's a bit sketchy, but over the last few years, she's made the rounds, even performed for some royal houses. Made some astonishing predictions, most of which turned out to be quite true. Married a very successful Russian businessman a few years ago, who tragically died less than a year later. And here's the really odd bit. Before her marriage, there's no record of her at all. He couldn't find a thing. It's as though she didn't exist before that."

"Curiouser and curiouser," Elizabeth said.

"It's possible she changed her name," Simon said. "Or the records were lost."

157

"Could be," Max agreed. "My friend's looking into it. He said he'd cable me again in the morning."

"Thank you," Elizabeth said. "That was very kind of you to do."

"My pleasure," he said with a courtly bow. "I don't suppose you'd like to tell me what this is all about? I'd like to help, if I can."

Elizabeth cast Simon a speculative glance.

"I do love a good adventure," Max added hopefully.

"I'm afraid it's nothing so exciting," Simon said. "Something for Lloyd's."

Max looked disappointed at that. "Insurance?"

"I'm afraid so. Some spurious claim. Just being diligent."

"That's a shame. I thought it might be something dangerous and exciting."

"No," Simon said with a quick look at Elizabeth. "Not dangerous or exciting at all."

"Try not to be too confrontational," Elizabeth said to Simon as they bumped along the road to Haight-Ashbury.

"Like you were with the Admiral."

Elizabeth made a sour face and looked out the window of the carriage. It was hard to believe that all of the amazing Victorian homes they passed would be rendered to nothing more than ashes and rubble in a just a few days. It made the breakfast she'd managed to get down that morning feel more like lead than toast.

Tomorrow was D-Day. She'd tried to remember every bit of information that Travers had told her. The trouble was, there wasn't much to remember. The details were sketchy at best. Graham was murdered sometime in the evening of Easter Sunday and time would be altered.

She glanced at Simon who was disturbingly undisturbed by the whole thing. If what the Council had said was true, history would change and one of those changes could affect Simon's very existence. And yet, he didn't seem worried. In fact, he looked quite at home. Maybe it was the dressy clothes or rights of privilege, but he seemed more confident somehow, more at ease. Whatever it was, the turn of the century suited him.

The carriage stopped in front of a group of lavish row houses, large two-story homes whose sides kissed. They were a little like the brownstones of New York, but the class was an upper not a lower.

Simon opened the door and helped Elizabeth out. 815 Ashbury. That's where Simon's contacts had said Madame Petrovka lived.

They walked up the steps to the portico and Simon rang the bell. A few seconds later Mr. Stryker, his craggy face as implacable as ever, opened the door.

"We'd like to see Madame Petrovka," Simon said.

Mr. Stryker gave them a small, hollow smile before stepping aside and letting them in. He asked them to wait in the parlor.

A few minutes later Madame Petrovka joined them. "I am not available for appointments today, but if you'd like to make arrangements with Mr. Stryker..."

"We'd like to talk to you about what happened at the Graham's," Simon said.

Madame Petrovka nodded and clasped her hands. "It was unusual. I cannot guarantee such—"

Simon grunted.

"A disbeliever. Yes, I sensed that the other evening," she said as she took a seat.

"Sensed it, did you?" Simon said and then cocked his head to the side. "Do you always drug your sitters?"

She shrugged. "The incense helps them relax. Some need it more than others."

Elizabeth knew she'd better jump in quickly before Simon got them kicked out. "It was amazing. And disturbing. What exactly happened?"

Madame Petrovka smiled. There was nothing ominous about the smile. It appeared completely genuine and yet it made Elizabeth shiver.

"Yes, wasn't it?" Madame Petrovka said. "Such a tragedy, losing a child like that."

Elizabeth could feel Simon winding up for a good one. "I felt something that night," she said quickly hoping to keep him from erupting. "I'm not sure how to describe it."

"Did you? You must be sensitive to the spiritual vibrations."

Elizabeth took Simon's hand in a silent appeal to play along. "What was it?"

"What did it feel like, my dear?"

Elizabeth knew this was a typical tactic by fraudulent mediums. She was doing all the talking, providing all the information and Madame Petrovka would keep providing the carrot as long Elizabeth was willing to play along. For now, she was. "Cold, very cold and…"

"Evil?"

Simon made another noise.

"I don't know," Elizabeth admitted. "I was hoping you could tell me."

"Of course you were." Madame Petrovka poured herself a cup of tea. "When a person dies their spirit begins a new journey through the realms to peace. Depending on how they lived their lives, spirits find themselves on different levels of ascendance. Sometimes, when a death is violent or life is filled with unresolved issues, the spirit can lose their way. Dear Violet is lost. Lost in a place with other souls that are tormented. It would be a horrible and frightening place for a child."

That made a disturbing sort of sense, even if Elizabeth didn't want it to. "And that other presence? Some sort of tortured soul or demon."

"Possibly."

"And I suppose for a price you'll help little Violet find peace," Simon said not bothering to hide his disdain.

"Simon—"

Madame Petrovka raised a hand. "It's quite all right. I'm used to it. Yes and no, Sir Simon. Yes, I do hope to help Violet find her way to the next realm and no, there is no price. She'd been abandoned. By the people she thought loved her," she said, the tenor of her voice and body language changing, tensing. "She was betrayed by them."

"Betrayed?" Elizabeth asked. Someone had lost the plot and she was pretty sure it wasn't her. From what she knew about the Grahams, they would never do anything to hurt their child. They loved Violet to distraction.

Madame Petrovka relaxed. "Perhaps I spoke too strongly. The child's spirit is quite powerful."

"And you're not taking any money from the Grahams for all of your…assistance?" Simon asked.

"Not a brass farthing, Sir Simon."

The room was chilly, but it wasn't anything supernatural.

Simon reached into his waistcoat pocket and pulled out the pocket watch. "We won't take up anymore of your time."

It was funny, Elizabeth hadn't even realized that the watch worked as a watch. She was about to say her goodbyes when she noticed that Madame Petrovka was staring intently at some nebulous spot on the wall. Elizabeth didn't see anything there and for a moment, Elizabeth thought the woman had fallen into a trance. Her eyes glassed over and she seemed almost to be in a fugue state. "Madame Petrovka?"

The woman took a deep breath. "My time. Yes. Time." She came back to herself and took a cleansing breath. "I do have appointments. If you'll see yourself out."

She almost hurried to the door, but turned back and smiled like the Cheshire Cat. "I'm so very glad you came."

MONIQUE MARTIN

CHAPTER NINETEEN

IT WAS HER TURN to watch. Elizabeth lay on her side; head propped up on her elbow and watched Simon sleep. She knew he often watched her as she slept. He said it was better than tea. From Simon, that was high praise.

How he could sleep at a time like this though, she had no idea. Tomorrow was Easter Sunday and unless she stopped whoever was after Victor Graham, everything she cared about would cease to be. As if he'd heard her, Simon gave a small snore and rolled his head to the side as he continued his blissful night's sleep. Amazing.

Was this what it felt like for Simon all those nights in New York? He'd had prescient nightmares of her death nearly every night. She'd been disturbed by them; who wouldn't, but she didn't really understand how he felt. Until now.

Their fight about her new job and her crappy car didn't just seem insignificant; they felt a lifetime away. In a way they were. What was it about traveling back in time that seemed to give them a fresh start? In New York it had given them a chance to fall in love and here, a chance to stay that way.

She rolled onto her back and tried to calm the torrent of possibilities that flooded her mind. There were just too many what ifs. How could she possibly protect Graham from all of them?

She kissed Simon's cheek, eased out of bed and pulled on her robe and slippers. Sleep wasn't going to come. Only two things helped and she and Simon had already tried the first. The second wasn't as surefire a method, but it was worth trying.

She picked up a candleholder and carefully made her way into the hall. She struck the match and lit the candle, but it wouldn't last long. It had nearly guttered out. She made her way downstairs protecting the flame as best she could.

The kitchen was bigger than she thought. As she moved to set her candle down and light the gas lamp when her candle gave up and the flame snuffed itself out. There were only a few windows in the kitchen and she had no idea where the matches were.

"Crud."

She was feeling her way along the edge of the table when the crack and sizzle of a match being lit broke the silence and a flickering light grew behind her.

"Trouble sleeping?"

Gerald, clad in his nightshirt, robe, slippers and nightcap looked like something straight out of *A Christmas Carol*. He held out the candle out between them.

"Lot on my mind," she said. "You?"

"I'm old."

She laughed and he lit the gas lamp and soon the room glowed with a yellow warmth. Elizabeth walked over to one of the cabinets and opened it. "Got anything to eat in this place?"

She opened a few more cabinets before Gerald stopped her. "Sit down. You'll just make a mess of things and I'm the one who'll have hell to pay with cook when she gets back. Just put that down and leave it to me."

He tossed his nightcap aside, took the can of kidney beans out of her hands and put it back in the cabinet. "I think we have some eggs," he said. "You can cut some bread for toast if you'd like."

"Eggs are fine."

He opened the icebox and pulled out a bowl of eggs, a bottle of milk and an ornate butter tray. "He still here?"

"Simon? Yes."

Gerald grunted, but no lecture followed.

Earlier that night, Elizabeth had pulled up her big girl panties and gone to see Mrs. Eldridge about Simon. She'd hemmed and hawed, as embarrassed as a teenager when Mrs. Eldridge had lowered her pince-nez and said, "I may be old, dear, but I'm not blind. I do remember what it feels like to be madly in love, you know. Life's far too short."

She'd said that she would ask Jane to make up a room for him for propriety's sake. She'd even promised to handle Gerald. And, judging from his response, or lack of one, she'd done just that.

Gerald bent down to revive the fire in the huge cast iron stove.

"Why do you hate him so much?"

He pushed some paper and kindling into the firebox and jabbed at the wood, forcing the flames to life.

"It's not him so much as…the English."

"All of them?"

"No," he said, "But when you've seen them do what I saw."

"Your leg?"

"That and more. I was good with a gun and twenty-two when the war started. My father and my uncles had all fought in the revolution and I saw my chance for glory."

"What revolution?"

He looked at her like she'd grown a second head. "For independence."

"That was over a hundred years ago."

"Are you going to keep interrupting or let me tell it?"

"I'm sorry." She really never would get used to things like this.

"It was 1813. The War of 1812. I don't suppose they teach about that when you come from?"

Elizabeth didn't mention the only thing she knew about the War of 1812 was a kitschy song from the fifties her father used to sing. It was a sobering thought that virtually an entire war had been swallowed by history. What else didn't they teach anymore?

"They came in the middle of the night," Gerald continued as he cooked. "Going to stick us with bayonets while we slept, but we gave them hell. Right in the middle of it, this man appears out of thin air. Magic. Everyone stopped, even the Brits."

He seemed lost in the memory for a moment before continuing. "But that didn't last long. One of them was about to shoot him in the back. That's how it was. I pulled him out of the way, stuck him behind a tree. I managed to shoot a few of them before I got my leg blown off a few minutes later."

Unconsciously, he rubbed the top of his thigh. "The last thing I remembered was the man looking down at me. They say I had fever for a week and when I finally woke up, I was here. Upstairs in this very house."

He plated the eggs and sat down.

"Mr. Eldridge was the man," Elizabeth said, knowing it was true.

"That was thirty years ago and I've been here ever since."

"Wow." Elizabeth tasted her eggs. "Good."

He raised his fork in salute.

She took another bite and discovered she really was hungry. "Thirty years. That's a long time to hold a grudge."

He eyed her carefully and smiled. "I have issues."

She laughed and after a few more bites, her egg was gone.

"Sleepy?" he asked.

She shook her head.

"Me neither," he admitted.

She really wasn't tired at all now. So much for Plan B. She rubbed the surface of the table, lost in thought, when she remembered that she had the perfect solution to sleepless nights. "You play cards, Gerald?"

"I've been known to."

"Any good?"

"Better than you, I'll wager."

Elizabeth smiled. "I'll take that bet."

They'd played for an hour before both headed back to bed. Sleep finally came for Elizabeth, but it was filled with haunting, disquieting dreams. The only comfort was waking up in Simon's arms.

After a quick breakfast they took Mrs. Eldridge's carriage to Simon's hotel so he could put on a fresh shirt and check in with his network of spies. Simon ran the entire thing with Machiavellian precision and a generous wallet. Anyone who learned anything useful reported back to the hotel concierge who, in turn, reported to Simon.

They picked up on Graham's trail as he left Easter services at the First Presbyterian Church. According to a valet at the Prescott mansion, the Grahams were scheduled to attend a lawn party there that afternoon, but their carriage traveled straight back to their house on Nob Hill.

Simon instructed their coachman to park across the street from the Graham's house, not so close as to draw suspicion, but close enough that they could see any comings and goings. They both settled in for a long wait.

They'd debated telling Graham that he was in danger, but without any proof at all it would have sounded slightly insane. They couldn't exactly tell him the truth either. Elizabeth had even suggested that they kidnap him and try to keep him safe that way, but

Simon had pointed out that they had no idea how he was killed or by whom. It was possible that their actions might even increase the danger to him. All they could do was watch and wait. And be ready to act when the moment came.

Elizabeth felt the carriage sway as the coachman climbed down from his seat. He brought a large wicker basket around that must have been stored in the rear compartment.

Simon took the basket and put it on the opposite seat. "Thank you, William."

When had he learned the coachman's name? And why hadn't she bothered to do the same?

Simon pulled the window shades down leaving just a sliver at the bottom to see through.

"What's this?" she asked, pointing at the large briefcase shaped basket.

"There's no telling how long we'll be here and it's best we're prepared for the duration."

He opened the basket to reveal bread, cheese, fruit, plates and utensils, even a thermos of something.

The hours passed with no movement in or out of the Graham's house. Simon stretched out his legs and propped them up next to the nearly empty basket on the far seat. He put his arm around Elizabeth and his long fingers brushed up and down her arm. It was strangely peaceful and Elizabeth felt herself melting into Simon's side. As far as stakeouts went, this wasn't so bad.

"What are you two doing here?"

Elizabeth and Simon jumped.

Teddy's face appeared in the window, his head ducking under the shade.

"Great googley moogley!" Elizabeth cried. "You nearly gave me a heart attack."

"I'm sorry," he said. He crammed his hand through the window and offered her his brown paper sack. "Peanut?"

"Teddy, please go home," Simon said.

Teddy pulled his arm back and pushed his head back into the cab. "Are you trying to be secret?"

"Yes, we are. So if you'd…"

"I have secrets," he said.

"Good," Simon said as though he were speaking to a small child. "Now, be a good chap and run along."

"I've been working on something, but things keep exploding."

"We'd love to hear about that," Elizabeth said as she tried to look past him to see if their cover had been blown. "But later."

Having Teddy hang off the side of their supposedly empty carriage wasn't exactly inconspicuous. "We'll come by later and see, all right?"

Teddy nodded. "Shhh," he whispered as he slipped out from under the shade and continued down the street.

Elizabeth fell back against her seat and shook her head.

"More of your magnetic personality at work?" Simon said. "I swear that you collect odd people the way some collect porcelain cats."

"It could be worse," she said.

Simon peaked under the shade to make sure Teddy had actually left. "How?"

"I could collect porcelain cats."

The afternoon turned into evening and evening into night. As the darkness came Elizabeth grew more anxious with every passing minute. She was exhausted and keyed up at the same time. It made her feel slightly queasy.

"What if it's already happened?" she said, "and we don't know."

"Then I wouldn't be here, would I?"

Elizabeth frowned. She hated the matter of fact way he said it.

"I'm sorry," he continued. "I know you're worried for me and I love you for it, but if I do...cease to be, you won't know to miss me, will you?"

"I'd know," she said almost angrily. "No matter what changed, I'd know."

He looked a little chagrined at that and brushed his knuckles along her jaw. "I believe you would."

"You haven't cornered the market on truly, madly, deeply, ya know? I do actually love you as much as you love me. You're not the only crazy person here."

He laughed and kissed her. "No indeed."

After another minute dragged by, she sat forward. "I can't just sit here anymore. I can't. I have to know what's going on in there."

She opened the carriage door and Simon put a hand on her arm. "All right," he said, pulling her back so he could exit first and help her out.

They walked over to the Graham's and rang the bell. After a moment, the maid answered.

"We're here to see Mr. and Mrs. Graham," Simon said.

The maid nodded and closed the door most of the way. They could hear voices inside and then Mary Graham appeared at the door. If it was possible, she looked even paler than she had before. "This isn't a good time."

"Are you all right?" Elizabeth tried to see inside. "Where's Mr. Graham?"

Mary pulled the door until it was barely a foot open. She was nervous and upset. "Victor's not feeling well."

"We'll send for a doctor. Perhaps we can help," Elizabeth said as she tried to ease the door open again. "Let us help you, Mary."

Mary looked like she was about to let them in when the door swung open and Victor Graham stared at them wild eyed. "You're not welcome here."

He was a shadow of the man he'd been that day at the Ferry building—his face unshaved, his clothes unkempt.

His eyes flared with anger. "She said you'd try to interfere."

"Who? Madame Petrovka?" Elizabeth asked.

"She's not what she appears to be," Simon said. "She's a fraud."

Graham shook his head violently. "Leave my house."

He tried to slam the door, but Simon held onto it. "You're not thinking clearly."

Graham turned to one his servants who watched the scene in horror. "Get the police. Now! Go!"

The footman scurried back into the house and disappeared.

"Victor, please," Mary said placing a hand on her husband's arm.

Victor shook her off. "Get inside."

Mary gave Simon and Elizabeth a look of apology and shame. "I'm sorry."

Victor turned back to Simon and Elizabeth. His eyes were bloodshot and painfully sad. His fury seemed to have burned itself out in an instant and he leaned against the door. "Please, just go."

"Let us help you," Elizabeth pleaded. "You're in danger."

Only the barest hint of hope lit his eyes before they went dull again. "Please?"

Simon let go of the door and Graham nodded his thanks before closing it in front of them. He led her back to their carriage.

"We can't just walk away."

Simon kept a hold of her arm. "Getting arrested isn't exactly going to help our cause, now is it?"

She couldn't argue with that, but how could she just sit and wait while Graham was coming unglued. They climbed back into the carriage and Elizabeth fidgeted.

Simon was deep in thought, staring out the window when he suddenly rapped hard on the roof of the cab. "We need to move. Now!"

"What's going on?"

Simon pointed to a buggy coming up the block. Inside was Victor Graham.

"But how?" Elizabeth asked.

"The servant's entrance. I'd completely forgotten about it until the footman ran to the back of the house to get the police." He opened the cab door and leaned out. "That carriage there, follow it."

As soon as Simon was back inside, their carriage took off after Graham. The streets were surprisingly busy for a Sunday night, but the traffic thinned quickly as they headed west away from town.

Elizabeth's heart pounded in time to the horse's hooves. Faster and faster. They passed Golden Gate Park and turned up the coast. They drove through the heights above the Cliff House and came to a rough dirt road that led further up the coast. Their carriage rolled to a stop. Elizabeth nearly cried out in frustration. They couldn't lose him now.

"Keep going," Simon called through the window.

"Can't, sir," William said. "That buggy can make it all right, but not the coach. We'll drop a wheel for sure."

Simon yanked open the door and helped Elizabeth. "You all right?" he asked.

She wasn't, but she nodded and they started down the dirt road on foot. It was tough going. The road was furrowed with deep ruts and chuckholes. Clouds blocked out most of the moonlight making the footing treacherous. Elizabeth clung to Simon's hand for balance as they ran down the road as quickly as they dared.

It wasn't long before the bushes and trees that lined the road gave way to a small open expanse. They found Graham's buggy abandoned at the base of a footpath that led further up the coast. In the distance, Elizabeth could just barely make out a figure in the darkness as it moved from shadow to shadow.

"There!"

She and Simon went after Graham, winding their way through the dense undergrowth, only catching glimpses of Graham as the path veered into the open. The ocean was close. She could taste the salt on the air and feel the cold, wet wind cutting through her clothes. They were somewhere along the bluffs above the sea, but she couldn't tell how far away it was.

The underbrush was thick and a clump of brambles caught her skirts and she nearly stumbled. With a few curses and rips she disentangled herself, but she knew she was slowing them down. Damn shoes and corset. She hated to do it, but there wasn't any choice. She would have ripped off all of her clothes if there'd been time, but there wasn't. Every second mattered. They couldn't afford to lose track of Graham now.

"Go after him," Elizabeth said. "I can't keep up."

"I won't leave you."

She grabbed him by the arms, pleading. "If you don't, I might lose you."

Simon hesitated, but Elizabeth pushed him ahead.

"Go. I'll be right behind you."

He nodded. "You'd better be." And then he disappeared into the brush ahead.

Cursing every fashion designer and shoemaker for the last one hundred years, Elizabeth followed behind as fast as she could. She stumbled and pricked her arm through the fabric of her sleeve. She ripped herself free and pushed on.

The bushes and trees thinned out and she could see that she was near the cliff's edge. Pushing her heart back down into her ribcage, she ran forward. The path serpentined through the woods, jigging one way and then another. Finally, the maze of woods ended abruptly and she emerged into the open air.

Somehow, she'd ended up about sixty feet back from the edge. In the mixture of rocks and grass in front of her, she saw Graham, farthest away, and Simon closing behind him. She thought it was just a shadow from a tree swaying in the wind, but then she realized that another man had stepped out of the darkness. He surged forward and raised something above his head. He was about to swing it down on Simon's head when she cried out.

"Look out!"

Simon reacted just in time to deflect the blow.

Elizabeth ran toward them, stumbling, cursing. She couldn't catch her breath and knew she was going to start hyperventilating soon, but she ran forward.

It was so dark she could barely tell where one man started and the other stopped as they fought. They fell to the ground and she lost them in the tall grass.

Graham continued his march to the sea cliff.

Somewhere ahead, Elizabeth heard grunting and panting. The grass rustled back and forth as the two men grappled with each other. She saw Simon stand and then the other man. It was Stryker. Was Madame Petrovka here too? As she turned to look for her, Stryker rushed toward her. Simon grabbed him by the arm and pulled him to the ground.

"Graham," Simon grunted as he wrestled with Stryker.

She spun around and saw him still walking toward the edge. With one last glance at Simon as he fought with Stryker, she ran toward Graham.

Graham had managed to walk out onto the very tip of a crag that jutted out above the roaring ocean below. As she got closer, the wind caught his voice and tossed it back to her. He was talking to someone.

"Don't be afraid," he said. "There's no reason to be afraid, darling."

"Victor!" Elizabeth called out. "Don't go any further."

"Don't cry, my darling," he said to the ocean. A great gust of wind came and nearly pushed him back. Elizabeth's heart lurched, but he stood firm.

His jacket fluttered wildly in the strong wind. One more step and he'd fall. One more gust and he'd fall. Dear God, he was going to fall. The rocks below were sharp and wet with ocean mist. She got down onto her knees and started to crawl out to him, desperate to reach to him. The jagged edges dug into her knees as she inched out toward him. "She's not there," Elizabeth yelled. "Violet is not there."

He seemed to notice her for the first time and turned to look back. "Don't you hear her?" he said.

Elizabeth shook her head, but then she heard it – the plaintive wails of a child crying. She shook her head. It was impossible. It must have been the wind. Please, Dear God, let it be the wind.

"It's a trick," Elizabeth said. She crawled on her hands and knees further out the escarpment. "Please, Victor, listen to me."

He turned back to face the sea. Frustration and desperation pushed her forward, but he was too far away and she was moving too slowly.

He reached out into the empty air. "Just take my hand, darling."

"Please," Elizabeth cried. He was only a few feet away now. She reached out just as he did.

"It'll be all right," Victor said calmly and then stepped off the cliff and fell into the darkness.

CHAPTER TWENTY

ELIZABETH CRIED OUT AS he fell. Graham's body hit the edge of the cliff and bounced out further toward the water. The seconds stretched out as he seemed to be falling in slow motion. Falling, falling and then, with a sickening thud, he hit the rocks.

She stared down at him in shock. His body lay bent and broken in a horribly unnatural way. The rough surf tugged at his jacket and his limp arm swayed back and forth with the pull of the current.

She felt a hot flush and tingling in her whole body. The icy wind bit into her face, but she could barely feel it. Her body was frozen in place. She couldn't wrap her mind around it. This wasn't supposed to happen. She was supposed to save him. To save...

"Simon!"

Elizabeth ignored the jagged rocks that tore into her hands and knees as she scrambled back from the edge. She quickly scanned the field, but didn't see him. He was here. She refused to believe he was gone. "Simon!" she called out again.

She ran back to the spot where she'd left him fighting with Stryker. He had to be here. He was here, she told herself over and over. He had to be here.

"Simon!"

She felt nauseous, dizzy, hot and cold at the same time. How could this have happened? How could she have let it happen? Panic tightened its grip on her as she ran back and forth through the tall grass. "Simon!"

Tears stung her eyes and blurred her vision. She'd failed. She'd lost him. She wiped the tears away angrily and choked back a sob. He couldn't be gone. He couldn't be. "Simon?"

"Elizabeth."

She spun around and just a few feet away in the grass stood Simon. Alive. Elizabeth's felt her knees actually buckle a little as relief flooded through her. He was alive. She faltered and then nearly knocked him down as she hugged him. "Oh, Simon," she said as she held on to him as tightly as she could. Tears burned her eyes and she could barely swallow. "I thought I'd lost you."

"Down but not out," he said rubbing the back of his head. He was a little groggy, but he was there. He was still with her. She kissed him again and again.

He pulled back from her and asked, "Graham?"

She shook her head and fought back a sob. "I couldn't stop him. He just... Simon, he just... walked off the edge. I tried, but..." The memory of it flashed back into her mind and she felt that cold iron fist clench in her stomach again. She tightened her grip on Simon's arms. "I don't understand, Simon, what happened? Graham's dead. Why didn't time change? Why...."

"Am I still here?" he finished.

She nodded; glad he'd said it and not her.

He touched her cheek. "I don't know, but I am. Are you all right?"

The memory of Graham falling flashed in her mind. Elizabeth winced and closed her eyes. "No. Yes. I think so. God, it was horrible."

Simon kissed the crown of her head and pulled her to him. "I'm sorry."

She was simply relishing being in his arms and his being in hers when she remembered. "Where's Stryker?"

"I don't know. We were fighting one minute, he hit me with something and then he just ran off. It's a little foggy. Was Petrovka here?"

"I don't know." Elizabeth felt the bump growing on the back of his head. "Ouch."

"It'll be all right. At least we can leave this place now. As long as..." He reached into his waistcoat and pulled out the watch. "As long as we have this."

Elizabeth wasn't quite so sure, but she kept her doubts to herself. At least they still had each other. Which, she realized with a pang, was more than Mary Graham had now. That poor woman.

Simon patted his pockets and frowned.

"What's wrong?" she asked.

"My gun."

"It probably fell out while you were fighting."

They searched for it, but it was too dark and the grass too dense.

"It's all right," Elizabeth finally said taking his hand. "We've got what matters."

By early morning they'd finished making their police report. They'd given the authorities every detail they could remember including everything they knew about Stryker's involvement. Shell shocked and spent, they rode back to Mrs. Eldridge's in silence. They tended to each other's cuts and bruises and crawled into bed.

As soon as they lay down in each other's arms, all of the adrenaline from the day started to wear off. Elizabeth felt raw and exhausted, but her mind wouldn't shut down. It spun with thoughts like cotton candy, gauzy and twisting away.

Was this all some ploy by the Council? Would Simon disappear when they returned to their own time? Would she ever stop seeing Graham's body hit the rocks?

Elizabeth burrowed her head into Simon's shoulder and tried to concentrate on the feeling of his chest beneath her hand, his arms holding her and the steady beat of his heart. Sleep came and withdrew, like waves lapping on the shore, until finally it pulled her all the way under.

Despite her fears, Simon was still there when she woke and back to his usual self.

"We can go south," Simon said over breakfast, "but we'll have to go past Monterey at the very least. Inland would better. Stockton should be far enough."

Elizabeth pushed a strawberry around her plate with her fork. She didn't want to go. Despite all of Simon's arguments, and there were plenty, she knew this wasn't over. There was something she was missing. Graham's death had to mean something.

The memory flashed into her head and she closed her eyes. Poor Victor. And poor Mary. Elizabeth still had Simon, but Mary Graham had lost her husband.

"We could go to Santa Barbara," Simon suggested. "See the old neighborhood. You'd like that."

"That could be interesting," she said half-heartedly.

Simon put down his teacup and fixed her with one of his patented Simon stares. "Elizabeth."

With that one simple word, so innocuous on the outside, Elizabeth felt her stomach tighten. Simon had a way with words.

Not so much the ones he chose to say, but the way he chose to say them. Her name could mean anything from "Thank God you're here, Dr. Wendell is boring me out of my skull" to "Don't you realize how gauche it is to put ketchup on your eggs?" And sometimes, like now, it was something that meant trouble.

"There's no rush, is there?" she said.

Simon raised an eyebrow. "No, of course not. One of the worst disasters in modern history is only two days away, but why rush?"

"There, you said it. Two days. As long as we leave the city by Tuesday night, we'll have plenty of time. That leaves us a whole day and a half."

Simon narrowed his eyes and looked like he was about to deliver a giant pinprick to her idea balloon, when he sighed and wiped his mouth with his napkin. "All right."

Elizabeth expected a fight, at the very least token resistance, but not complete and immediate submission. It was suspicious.

He must have read her expression because he smiled and said, "No tricks. I'm trying to be supportive. Even if it is a foolish and unnecessary risk."

She smiled. That was the Simon knew and loved.

"But you have to promise me," he continued. "We will leave this city no later than Tuesday evening. No arguments."

"Deal."

"Good."

"By the way, I've already spoken Mrs. Eldridge about the earthquake," Elizabeth said and immediately held up a hand to stave off Simon's rebuke. "But, apparently, I didn't need to. Her husband had already told her about it."

"Good, when is she leaving? I assume she's taking that idiot nephew with her."

"She's not. I tried to tell her what it was going to be like, but she said that she wanted to stay and help. At least we know the house survives the earthquake. Her husband assured her it would. I don't know about the fires though."

"I'm afraid not very much survived the fires."

"I'll talk to her again," Elizabeth said taking a bite of her elusive strawberry. "But she's stubborn."

"Is she?" Simon said with a smirk. "So, pray tell, what exactly do you plan on doing with your reprieve?"

Elizabeth put her napkin on the table and pushed back her chair. Simon stood and pulled out her chair for her.

"I'm going for a walk," she said. "Have some noodling to do."

"In that case," Simon said. "I think I'll pay Harrington a visit."

Elizabeth arched an eyebrow.

"And see what else his contacts have found out about Madame Petrovka," Simon continued. "We should also check on Mary Graham later today. I'm sure she'd welcome any support she can get. We might not have been able to save Graham, but we might be able to save Petrovka's next victim from the same fate."

Elizabeth slipped her arms around his waist. "You're a big softy."

He pulled her closer. "No reason to be insulting."

She kissed his cheek. "Your secret is safe with me."

"I've got a secret!"

Elizabeth jumped at the voice. "Teddy! You've got to stop doing that."

She'd gone out for a walk through the quiet streets of Nob Hill and was completely lost in her thoughts when Teddy had appeared at her side.

"I'm sorry," he said, obviously having no idea what he was apologizing for.

"It's all right," she said. It was impossible to stay angry with Teddy. "So you have a secret?"

"It's amazing!" he shouted, like a ten year old who just got his first Xbox.

Elizabeth laughed. "Shhh. It won't be a secret if you shout about it like that."

"It's amazing," he whispered. "Do you want to see it?"

From any other man that would have been a painful come-on, a bit like "come see my etchings", wink-wink. She giggled again, this was probably exactly the time when men actually did use that line.

Teddy giggled along with her.

She thought about begging off, but maybe a distraction would do her good. She wasn't getting anywhere as it was. She just kept going over the same ground and each pass left her with a bigger ball of angst in her stomach and no answers. "I'd love to see your secret."

Teddy's entire body seemed to smile. She slipped her arm through his and he stared at it before standing a little taller and escorting her down the street.

The Fiske house rivaled the Graham's. It was large and imposing and everything Teddy wasn't. The door opened even before they reached it. She wondered for a moment if it was triggered automatically but then she saw a little old butler try to push it closed. The man wasn't just old; he was "there's probably a picture of Moses in his high school yearbook" old. He creaked along and Teddy stepped forward to help him close the front door. Once it was secure, he helped the old man shuffle over to a large plush chair that sat oddly in the middle of the hallway.

"Do you need anything, Donald?" Teddy yelled.

The man frowned, held up an ear trumpet and Teddy yelled the question again. Donald shook his head and Teddy patted his shoulder before turning back to Elizabeth. "Down here."

He led her down the hall and into the library. It was the kind of room Elizabeth had always dreamt of. Books covered the walls from floor to high ceiling. There was even an upper level complete with a walkway and railing that circled the perimeter of the room. A ridiculously large rich, ornate Oriental rug covered the floor and huge squishy dark leather chairs sat under large streetlamp-like lights in the corners.

"This," she said, "is heaven on Earth. If Simon saw this he would have had serious book-envy."

"Over here," he said resting his hand on the gilded edges of a book called *Memoirs of the Twentieth Century*. He flattened his hand along the spine and pushed. The entire wall swiveled. Teddy reached inside the opening and turned a wall switch. A weak overhead light struggled to life and illuminated the secret passage behind.

"You are full of surprises," Elizabeth said as she followed him down the dim corridor.

At the end of the short hallway, there was another door. This one was thick steel, like a vault door with two large locks and a combination tumbler. Teddy dug a key ring from his pocket and undid the locks and spun the dial of the tumbler. He put his hand on the door handle and then turned back to Elizabeth. "This is our secret now. And you can't tell anyone."

She promised.

He pulled the door open and added, "They wouldn't understand."

She didn't like the sound of that, but she followed him through the passage and down a rickety winding staircase into the dark room below. The light from the hall faded behind them and she had to grip the railing to keep her footing. Wherever they were going it was big. She could hear the way their footsteps echoed into the chamber.

"Can you turn on a light?" she asked.

"Right," he said and then she heard metal scraping against metal and a loud pop. An electrical hum built in intensity and then large overhead lights sparked to life.

She blinked to adjust to the sudden brightness and stood gaping at what she saw. The room was big, but it wasn't the size that stunned her. It was the four giant Tesla coils and circular metal cage. It was the racks of equipment with dials and gages. It was the tables full of Bunsen burners and beakers and bubbling liquids.

Teddy was a mad scientist.

Chapter Twenty-One

Elizabeth stepped uncertainly into the giant room. She knew Teddy was quirky, but this way, way beyond quirky. This was "on the government watch-list" quirky.

"What is all this?" she asked.

"My experiments," he said, puffing out his chest. He ushered her over to a table covered with blueprints, drawings and schematics and dug through a stack of graphs and maps.

Teddy mumbled to himself and finally pulled out a copper-colored ball from beneath the stack of papers. It was about the size of a baseball. "Eureka! Archimedes said that. Did you know that Archimedes claimed he could lift the earth if he had something to stand on? I'd like to see that. Wouldn't you like to see that?"

"Yes, that would be something to see." Elizabeth said and then gestured to the ball in his hands. "What is that?"

Teddy cocked his head to the side. "A ball."

"I mean what does it do?"

He smiled. "You'll see."

Elizabeth was all for adventure, but judging from the bookcase along one wall whose shelves were filled with things she couldn't identify floating in formaldehyde, maybe a little caution wouldn't be a bad thing. The scorch marks on the opposite wall weren't exactly comforting either.

"Over here," Teddy said.

She joined him by a large bank of dials and switches.

"Are those really Tesla coils?" she asked. She'd seen pictures of them in books, but never in person. These were about 15 feet high with metal cages around the base and a large sort of flying saucer thing on top.

"Of a sort. I...I redesigned them. His could create power, but they didn't harness it in the same way these do. It...it focuses," he said wiggling his hands in the air. "Concentrated and the electro-magnetic field is more stable. Usually."

"Usually?"

He handed her the copper colored ball and added, "It might get a little loud."

He pulled on a series of levers and switches and one by one the giant coils came to life. Each large metal tower began to spark in turn. Tendrils of electricity arced out from the big metal donut at the top of the tower and out into space like bright blue snakes. It was all oddly familiar. Each tower's electrical arc connected with the next until there was a canopy of crackling blue energy above them.

"This way," Teddy yelled.

He led Elizabeth over to the large metal cage that sat in the middle of the room. As the electrical storm raged above them, an occasional loud crack made Elizabeth cringe and duck.

"Is this safe?" she yelled.

He nodded. "It's been over a week since anything exploded."

Elizabeth forced a smile. "Good."

He climbed two steps up to the large metal cage and opened the door. The cage itself was big enough for three or four people to stand comfortably inside and had a console with a complex instrument panel. He waved for her to follow him inside.

It was madness. Teddy, who helped her up the steps, was clearly mad. She knew as she closed the gate behind her that she had to be mad for even considering it. And Simon would be an entirely different kind of mad when he found out what she'd done.

"Ready?" Teddy asked as he adjusted a few dials.

"For what?"

"My secret," he said as he dropped the copper-colored ball into a hollow cylinder in the control panel.

He held out his hand to her. "Hold on tight."

The humming and crackling grew louder and louder. The electric arcs reached toward them and surrounded the cage. Holding on tight would not be a problem.

A frighteningly familiar sensation took root in the pit of her stomach. She looked at Teddy in surprise. Only one thing felt like that. She knew what would come next—the incredibly disconcerting feeling of complete paralysis and then the world would shake itself apart around them. And it did.

When Elizabeth came back to herself she was standing outside. She could feel the sun on her face and hear a crowd and a...band? It took a moment to clear her head and when she did she knew exactly where and, more importantly, when she was.

The crowd gathered at the base of the stage in front of the Ferry Building and sang along with a brass band as it played "Bill Bailey". She looked to the side of the stage and saw Max meeting Teddy and shaking his hand. And then she saw herself. They'd traveled back in time.

Teddy was the watchmaker.

The Teddy next to her started to hum. "I like this song."

"How did you?" Elizabeth stammered, trying to break away from the incredibly odd sensation of watching herself. And it wasn't just that that muddled her brain. This meant that not only was Teddy linked to the Council, he'd somehow managed to break one of their cardinal rules. No time travel within your own lifetime. "I didn't think it was possible."

"Anything's possible," Teddy said as he hummed along. "Why do you think he doesn't want to come home?"

"Who?"

"Bill Bailey."

She was about to ask another question when the familiar feeling started in her stomach again.

"Oh, here we go," Teddy said tightening his grip on her hand. "Automatic return."

They reappeared inside the metal cage. The sudden shift from the relative quiet of Market Street to the cacophony inside Teddy's lab made Elizabeth flinch. Teddy held on tightly to her hand and flipped a few switches. The copper ball popped out and slowly the coils began to shut down. Her stomach roiled and her head had already started to throb.

Once the arcs had stopped he let go of her. "Did you like it?"

Her mind was reeling. Was Teddy the start of the Council? Was she the start of it? "This is big," Elizabeth said to herself. Even through her fuzzy brain she knew something incredibly important had just happened.

"I'm trying to make it smaller."

"I didn't mean—"

Teddy opened the cage door and they stepped out. "Maybe something you can carry."

"Like a watch?" Elizabeth said absently.

Teddy's eyes lit up. "Yes. A watch! I like that."

Oh, boy. She really had to be more carful. "Does anyone know about this?"

"Just you. It's our secret, remember?"

"And it's one hell of a secret, Teddy."

Elizabeth was wearing a hole in Mrs. Eldridge's very fine Persian rug when Simon returned from his fact-finding mission.

"Didn't learn much about our Madame Petrovka," he said, "but we did discover some interesting things about that man Stryker."

"You don't know from interesting," Elizabeth said under her breath. After seeing Simon's frown, she added, "I found something out myself. You go first."

"We took a chance and enquired about Stryker and it seems he has a rather colorful past. He was arrested several times for petty theft and other minor infractions and then sometime in his twenties he grew increasingly violent until he murdered a man. In 1882 he was admitted to Bethlam Royal Hospital, more commonly known as Bedlam."

"The insane asylum?"

"Yes. And despite being a murderer, and having committed multiple heinous acts during his stay in the hospital, he was released. A mysterious and quite wealthy patron apparently secured it."

"Paid for it?"

"Yes."

"I think we're safe to assume Madame Petrovka was his mysterious benefactor."

"But why would she do it?" Elizabeth asked. "How would she even know about a man like that?"

"Perhaps they knew each other before. Her past is still a mystery. I'd venture to say though that their paths crossed far before his release." Simon sat down on the sofa and stretched his long legs out in front of him. "We've got enquiries out about that. But, I don't know if they'll find anything in time."

Right. Time. In just under 48 hours, San Francisco would fall apart. Literally. Would Teddy's underground laboratory survive? Would Teddy? Mrs. Eldridge? Would anyone she'd met?

"What's wrong?" Simon asked.

She followed Simon's gaze and realized she'd nearly destroyed one of the couch pillows by picking at a loose seam. She poked some stuffing back in and put it aside.

"I hate that we can't change things and yet, I'm kind of afraid I did."

"Elizabeth, what did you do?"

"Nothing, maybe. Or, maybe, I might have said something that's sort of responsible for the beginnings of the inklings of the founding of the Temporal Council and the invention of the time traveling watch."

"I was gone two hours."

She shrugged. "It was an interesting two hours."

She proceeded to tell him about her adventure with Teddy and needlessly, swore him to secrecy.

"Teddy? Teddy Fiske discovered time travel?" Simon said as he prowled the edge of the room, still trying to process what she'd told him. He rubbed the back of his neck and shook his head. "Do you have any idea how dangerous what you did was?"

"I didn't know we were going to time travel."

Simon narrowed his eyes. "And if you'd known?"

He had her there and they both knew it.

Simon sighed dramatically. "Elizabeth. Experimental time travel and, worse yet, traveling into your own past."

"I told Teddy that wasn't kosher."

"Oh, well, in that case," Simon said with a sarcastic air of nonchalance. "Elizabeth," he breathed out as he sat down heavily onto the sofa.

"It seemed like the right thing to do." And it had. If the powers that be wanted her to do or not do something they needed to send out a memo.

Simon was quiet for a moment and Elizabeth braced herself for another talking to, but Simon seemed to have shifted gears without notice.

"When Travers came to see you," he said, "he said that everything that happened in 1929 was meant to be."

"Yeah…"

"Perhaps your interaction with Teddy was also meant to be. We know the watches already exist because we have them, so someone must have created them. We wouldn't have been able to come back here if that wasn't already the case."

Elizabeth plopped down onto the sofa next to him and rubbed her temples. "I'm getting one of those paradox headaches."

"It is a bit confusing, isn't it? We simply have to assume that everything we've done here is meant to be. That we're not changing time."

"You're forgetting the fact that we were sent here to do just that by saving Graham."

"And yet, we didn't. Graham still died."

"But that's a change, isn't it? In the original timeline, he wasn't supposed to die and when he did, time changed. Or did it?"

Elizabeth scrunched up her face in discomfort. "I need some seltzer or something. Time travel upsets my stomach."

Simon stood and pulled the velvet cord by the fireplace that summoned one of the servants.

"I know you don't believe the Council," Elizabeth said, ignoring Simon's acid expression, "but what if they were right about time changing, just not about how."

"Go on," Simon prompted.

A knock on the salon door interrupted her reply and the maid Jane stepped in.

"Miss Elizabeth isn't feeling well. Is there something on hand for an upset stomach?" Simon asked.

Jane nibbled her lip, bobbed her head and blushed. "Is it a womanly thing, Miss?"

Elizabeth snorted delicately and shook her head. "No, just a bit nauseous. Some crackers would be lovely, if you have them."

Jane dipped a quick curtsey and left.

"Womanly problems?" Elizabeth said with a giggle that died in her throat. The proverbial penny dropped like a cartoon anvil. "Womanly problems. Simon! I've got it. I think I know what's happened. Graham's death was supposed to destroy his family tree and all of his descendants. But it didn't."

"We've established that," Simon said.

"Because it was too late. The seed's already been planted, Simon. Mary Graham isn't sick; she's pregnant."

Chapter Twenty-Two

"**A**RE YOU SURE?" SIMON asked.

"No, but it makes sense, doesn't it?"

Simon nodded thoughtfully and ran his fingers through his hair, finding the bump on the back of his head still tender.

"And if it's true, Mary is in serious danger."

"Not necessarily," Simon said. "She could lose the child naturally."

"Aren't you a ray of sunshine?"

Simon hated to point it out, but they needed to try to keep clear heads about all of this. "It is unpleasant to contemplate, but the reality is that the infant and mother mortality rates are still painfully high at this time. It's also possible the child survives the birth only to fall victim to Diphtheria, Influenza, an accident or any of a dozen things. Including, need I remind you, a rather devastating earthquake."

"That's true," Elizabeth said crestfallen. "I hate it when you make a good point."

"But," Simon said and smiled as Elizabeth immediately perked up. "It would be prudent to see if we can't convince Mrs. Graham to leave town."

"Hooray for prudent!"

Simon shook his head and stood. He held out his hand to Elizabeth and he helped her up. "We don't have long. We'd better be convincing."

Elizabeth had a look in her eye Simon knew too well. Mary Graham had no idea what she was up against.

"She'll leave."

The black mourning dress made Mary Graham's already sallow skin look almost translucent. "I can't leave."

She sat in the same chair she had the last time they'd visited her. Was it really just a few days ago? That had been difficult enough; now the poor woman wasn't just mourning the loss of a child, but her husband as well.

"It isn't safe here," Simon said. "I'm afraid your husband's death wasn't an accident."

Mary closed her eyes in anguish and took a moment to compose herself before answering in a hoarse whisper. "I know."

Elizabeth moved to the edge of her seat. "Then you have to see that it's dangerous for you stay." Mary shook her head, but Elizabeth pressed on. "For you and your baby."

Mary Graham looked as though she was going to deny it, but instead she smiled sadly. "Victor didn't even know. I was going to tell him, but I wanted to make sure. I...I've miscarried before, you see, and each time a part of Victor...I wanted to be sure this time and now it doesn't matter at all."

Mary broke down into tears and Simon felt thoroughly helpless. Thankfully, Elizabeth joined Mary on the settee and took her hand. "It does matter. More than you know."

Mary sniffled and wiped her tears. "I still can't leave. There's an inquest into Victor's…and there are funeral arrangements to be made. I…"

"Just for a few days," Elizabeth said.

"Why would she want to hurt Victor that way? What could we possibly have done to her to make her hate us so?"

Simon leaned forward in his chair. "You didn't do anything, Mrs. Graham. You're not to blame in this."

"It was as though she'd cast some sort of spell on him," Mary said. "Did you know that he saw her several times after the séance? She claimed she could help us save Violet. I…I didn't believe her, but Victor was convinced. He thought she was our only hope. Is she some sort of witch?"

"No," Simon said quickly, staving off anything Elizabeth might have said to the contrary. "Not a witch. Just a very sick woman."

"Please reconsider, Mary," Elizabeth said. "Simon and I will take you wherever you want to go. Just for a few days."

A knock on the door interrupted them. The Graham's butler stepped in. "Pardon the intrusion, ma'am, but the police are here."

"Oh, yes, please bring them in," Mary said and then turned to Simon and Elizabeth. "I'm sorry, but I just can't leave."

Two blue-coated policemen stepped into the parlor. "Ma'am," one of them said curtly before addressing Simon. "Are you Sir Simon Cross?"

Simon hesitated. "Yes."

"You need to come with us, sir."

"What's going on?" Elizabeth crossed the room and tried to put herself between Simon and the officers.

"Please step aside, Miss," one of them said.

Simon had a sinking feeling about this.

"Not until you tell me what's going on," she demanded.

"His lordship is under arrest," the officer said and held up a pair of heavy iron cuffs. "Now, step aside before I clamp a pair of these on you too, Miss."

Elizabeth didn't budge.

"It's all right, Elizabeth," Simon said with much more confidence than he felt. "I'm sure there's just been some sort of misunderstanding."

"Not unless you count murder as a misunderstanding," the officer said as he put the cuffs on Simon's wrists. "You, sir, are under arrest for the murder of Victor Graham."

The jail cells at City Hall were probably just about as clean as the stables at City Hall. Something resembling a mattress was thrown on top of a metal platform that was suspended by heavy chains from the wall. Simon could only imagine the lice, bedbugs and God only knew what else that were living inside it. The only other decoration in his eight by eight foot cell was a bucket in the corner. The stench coming from it was overwhelming.

And yet, the worst part of it was the walls. Not because they pressed in on him, which they did, but because they were made of brick. Each one would be a potential death sentence when the earthquake came, and it was coming closer with every passing minute. He had to get out of this wretched place before then.

He reached for his watch and then remembered that it and everything else he'd had with him was locked away in that damned enormous filing cabinet across the room in the office area. If he managed to break out, he'd have to break into that. It wouldn't be easy either. This wasn't a typical office filing cabinet. Of course, breaking out or breaking in, neither seemed all that likely at the moment.

The bars to his cell were made of heavy iron. There was no way he could break through them. He was trapped. Good and well trapped. He slammed his hand hard against them and heard a loud rumbling snore from the cell next to his.

"Perfect."

He heard voices in the hallway – Elizabeth and two men. She appeared in the doorway and he was struck by how badly he'd needed to see her. She hurried across the room and met him at the bars. Behind her, Max slipped a handful of bills into a policeman's hand.

The officer looked around and said, "Five minutes."

Max nodded, shoed the officer out and then leaned against the door jamb.

Elizabeth wrapped her hands around Simon's. "Are you all right?"

"What's this all about?"

Elizabeth's eyes grew even more worried. "It seems Victor didn't fall to his death."

"I don't understand."

"He was shot."

"That's absurd, we told them what happened."

Elizabeth paced around the small room. "I know. They said because the body was badly damaged it took time for them to discover the bullet wound."

"That's absurd." Simon had a horrible feeling that he knew where this was headed.

"It gets better. Your gun was found on the rocks near the body."

"Stryker." Simon had thought he'd lost it in the tall grass, but Stryker must have taken it while they were fighting. "That's hardly enough evidence for an arrest. How did they even know the gun's mine?"

"You apparently 'waved it around' in Chinatown and made quite an impression on the locals."

"That's ridiculous."

"But wait, there's more," Elizabeth said. "Several witnesses including most of the Graham's household staff and a few neighbors saw you arguing with Graham the night before he died. He even had to send one of his servants to get the police because you wouldn't leave him alone."

This was not looking good, not good at all. Simon felt those brick walls closing in just a little bit with each passing second.

"And then," Elizabeth continued, "you followed him to Land's End. They said I was lucky that I hadn't been arrested as an accomplice."

Simon's head was spinning. "Quite a neat little web. And I seem to be stuck right in the middle of it."

Elizabeth came to his side, reached through the bars and took his hand. "We'll find a way out of this, out of here. It's what we do, remember?"

Dear, wonderful Elizabeth. How he loved her. As much as he believed they could find a way to exonerate him, it wouldn't happen fast enough. He was trussed up as neatly a Christmas goose. "I want you to promise me something."

"I don't like the sound of that."

"If you can't secure my release by tomorrow night, I want you to leave this city."

"No can do."

He knew she'd balk at that, but he pressed on. "Elizabeth, I'm serious about this."

She touched his cheek. "I know you are."

He took her hand and held it between both of his. She needed to understand. "Listen to me. I need to know you'll be safe. That matters more to me than anything else in this world."

"I know."

She was maddening. "Then you'll go?"

"We didn't come here together," she said, "but we're leaving that way. One way or the other"

"Don't be so damned noble."

"Said the martyr."

She was impossible. If he had to he'd find a way to have her kidnapped and… "Harrington."

"Oh no, you don't," Elizabeth said. "Leave him out of this."

"Harrington," Simon said, "if you truly have feelings for Elizabeth—"

"Hello!" Elizabeth said. "Grown woman. Making up her own mind."

Simon heaved a defeated sigh. "You're impossible." He caught Harrington's eyes and said, "Just watch over her, would you?"

Max nodded and in that instant an understanding passed between the two men.

Elizabeth threw up her hands and shook her head. "You two make your caveman compact. That's fine. This helpless little damsel is going to find a way to get your ass out of here. That is, if I have your permission, Sir Simon?"

Despite the situation, Simon laughed. She was so wonderfully alive and beautiful when she was angry. "Elizabeth…"

Her pique melted away as fast as it had come and she walked over to his cell again. "I love you," she said.

"Just promise me you'll be careful."

"Aren't I always?"

Chapter Twenty-Three

Elizabeth had promised Simon that she'd be careful. Then she'd promised Max the same when he'd brought her home. All she needed was for Gerald to come in and she'd have a trifecta. Not that it mattered what she promised them; if recklessness was what it took, she was prepared to be a raving maniac.

Simon might have to spend tonight in jail, but tomorrow, she'd find a way. The trouble was, she had no idea where to start.

Madame Petrovka had Simon tied up with a pretty ribbon. She'd obviously manufactured the witnesses from Chinatown and heaven only knew who else she had on her payroll.

No matter how many times Elizabeth went over it in her head, every path seemed blocked to her and even those that might pay off, would take too damn long. She thought about kidnapping Mary Graham, at least that might give Simon a chance. But she knew it wasn't enough. She'd lived in California long enough to know what kind of building could survive an earthquake and City Hall wasn't one of them. And even if she did somehow manage to break Simon out of jail, he could still die if Madame Petrovka got her hands on Mary Graham and her baby.

No matter which move she made, the other left her Simon at risk. But nothing was impossible. There had to be a way.

She paced the length of the salon and looked at the clock on the mantle—nearly midnight. She did some quick calculations. The quake struck just after 5 a.m. the day after next. That gave her twenty-nine hours, twenty-eight if they wanted a chance to get out of the city.

"Twenty-eight hours," she said to the empty room. It could have been twice as long, three times, and she'd still be just as stuck. For the first time in a very long time, Elizabeth had no idea what to do next.

The front doorbell rang and startled her from her funk. She peeked through the bay window into the darkness to see who it was. Teddy stood on the stoop repeatedly touching a leaf from a nearby bush.

Gerald let him in and Teddy came bounding into the salon. "Hi!"

"Hi, Teddy." She flopped down onto the sofa and stared into the fire. "What are you doing here?"

"Max told me what happened and I want to help."

"I wish you could."

Teddy looked around anxiously and then joined her on the sofa. He scooched closer until their legs were touching and then he leaned in and whispered, "Our secret can help."

"What do you—"

"I can go back. I've never tried to change anything, but I bet I could."

Elizabeth felt a rush of temptation that would have put Lot's wife to shame. It could work. Just something small. They didn't have to change anything significant, just a message from herself to herself. That would certainly put a different spin on "if I only knew then what I know now", wouldn't it? What harm could it do?

She could save Simon. She could even save Graham. Even Captain Picard bent the Prime Directive every once in a while.

She was just about to agree to it when she looked into Teddy's face, his completely guileless face. And she knew it was wrong. Oh, it was tempting. So damned tempting. But it was wrong, so very wrong. She knew it as surely as anything she'd ever known. She couldn't do it.

"Thank you, Teddy. That's sweet of you, but that's a very, very dangerous path. I don't think either of us is qualified to play God, do you?"

Teddy's beard wiggled as he chewed his lip deep in thought. Finally, he shook his head. "No. But I still want to help. I'd give you the moon if I could."

He was so dear and Elizabeth wanted help, but what could he do? There had to be something. He was a genius, after all. A crazy mad genius with scorch marks on the wall of his laboratory.

"I think there is something you can do."

He brightened.

Elizabeth grinned back. "How would you like to blow something up?"

Elizabeth and Teddy strategized into the wee hours of the morning. The next morning, Max was already there when Elizabeth came downstairs.

"What's the plan?" he said.

As much as she wanted his help, she felt a pang of guilt. He had no idea what the next 24 hours held. "It could get dangerous," she said in epic understatement.

Max grinned. "I eat danger for breakfast."

"I'm serious, Max."

His smile faded and he looked, for the first time since she'd met him, like a man and not a playboy. "I know you are. I don't claim to understand what's going on, but I do know that this is something I'd like to see through to the end. For once," he said self-deprecatingly. "No matter where it leads."

She took his hand. "You're a good friend, Max."

He smiled again, but she saw the pain behind it. "Come on, then," he said. "Where do we start?"

They went to see Simon first. He looked the way she felt.

"You don't happen to have a toothbrush with you, by any chance?" he said. "I think they serve actual gruel here."

"Sorry, no toothbrush, something better."

Max was still arguing with the guard. They'd brought a parcel for Simon, but the guard wouldn't let them pass with it.

"It's cheese," Max said.

The guard pointed at the package. "Open it up."

"All right," Max said, "but don't say I didn't warn you."

Max untied the strings to the brown paper and unwrapped a block of Limburger cheese. He shoved it toward the guard who winced and covered his nose with his sleeve.

"Cover it up," the guard said. "People actually eat that?"

"English," Max said with a nod over his shoulder and a shake of his head.

The guard seemed to find that an adequate explanation. He nodded and held out his hand. Max greased his palm with another small bribe and the guard left them alone.

"Who says corruption's a bad thing?" Max said.

Elizabeth took the package from him and slipped it through the bars to Simon. "This is for later. When you're alone."

She asked him about his guards, how many there were, when they checked the room. Anything he could tell her about their patterns, numbers and locations. They were lucky in that it appeared the police felt their City Hall jail was inescapable and didn't guard the prisoners very carefully. And why should they? The outer walls were thick masonry with two layers of bricks.

Simon said that last night a guard had checked on him around two or three a.m., he couldn't be sure. And then they didn't return until after dawn, probably closer to six a.m. That was pushing it, but they could make it work. They had to.

Other than being cranky about his lack of tea, Simon appeared to be absurdly calm. But she knew him better than that and could see the worry in his eyes. She kissed him and told him not to worry. It was a stupid thing to say. How could either of them not worry? But she said it and he said it back to her and there was some strange comfort in it even if neither really believed what the other was saying.

The next stop was the Graham's. She had to try one more time to convince Mary Graham to leave. However, when they arrived the butler told them that his mistress wasn't at home. She'd received a telephone call early that morning and left without telling anyone where she was going.

Elizabeth could feel the ball in the pit of stomach start to spin. She knew where she'd gone, just not why, although now it hardly mattered. Madame Petrovka could have threatened her or promised her something and in Mary's state she might have believed anything.

But maybe it wasn't too late. She and Max hurried across town to the Haight and Madame Petrovka's. If Elizabeth could find out what she wanted maybe she could make a deal for Mary's life. That is if Mary was still alive. The ball in her stomach dropped at the thought.

She and Max pounded on the front door and Mr. Stryker invited them inside as if they'd shown up for tea. But when he opened the door to the salon, he blocked Max's path.

"You wait here," he said. "The girl can go in."

"I'm sorry, but that's not possible." Max stepped around Stryker, but the small man was fast and jabbed a crooked finger into Max's chest. "I said, you wait."

"It's all right," Elizabeth said, knowing it wasn't.

"I'll be right out here," Max assured her as he shoved Stryker's hand off his chest.

Stryker smiled that awful yellow smile of his. "Good lad."

Elizabeth walked into the salon and the door closed behind her. Madame Petrovka reclined casually in a large chair rolling a coin in her fingers and then palming it.

"Where is she?" Elizabeth demanded.

"Please, sit down." Madame Petrovka rolled the coin one more time and then it vanished from her hand. She waved it with a flourish. Elizabeth was not impressed.

"Where is Mary Graham?"

"She's safe." She must have seen the wheels in Elizabeth's head turning, imagining the layout of the house. "Not here, of course. That would be careless. Now, please sit."

Elizabeth sat down stiffly. She tried not to let the relief show on her face. Mary was still alive. Simon still had a chance.

"So much more civilized. When you've experienced what I have, you learn to appreciate the small courtesies." Madame Petrovka poured tea as she spoke. "Tea?"

Elizabeth shook her head. "Just Mary, thanks."

Madame Petrovka ignored that remark. "I think it's only fair since I've answered your question, that you should answer one of mine."

When Madame Petrovka spoke again, all traces of her Russian accent were gone. She sounded almost like she was from the mid-west. "Why do you care? What are the Graham's to you?"

"That's two questions," Elizabeth said. "But the answer is the same for both. I don't like to see someone, anyone, manipulated and abused."

Madame Petrovka laughed. "Manipulated and abused?" Her laughter stopped abruptly and her demeanor shifted from curious to intense and more than a little frightening. "You have no idea what those words really mean."

Elizabeth wasn't about to be intimidated. Not now, with everything on the line. "I don't know what happened to you or what you think happened to you—"

"Don't you? I thought everyone in the Council would know by now. Or did Charles lie about that too?"

Elizabeth's fingernails dug into the fabric of the sofa cushion and she struggled to keep her voice calm. "The Council?"

"How did they find me?"

Sweet Aunt Jabippy. What did Petrovka have to do with the Council? "I don't know what you mean."

"Don't lie to me!" Madame Petrovka's eyes grew unnaturally dark for a moment and Elizabeth could feel the air grow instantly cold. "I saw the watch."

Oh, this was not good. Definitely not good. Elizabeth waited until the storm seemed to have passed. Madame Petrovka was either crazy or possessed or both and worse yet, she knew about time travel and the Council. Time for a change of tactics. "How do you know about that?"

Madame Petrovka huffed impatiently. "The same as you do, my dear. I'm one of them."

Elizabeth struggled to maintain her composure. Of all the things Elizabeth had expected that wasn't one of them. Travers hasn't said anything about another time traveler. It made her wonder what else he'd conveniently left out.

"Or at least I was," Madame Petrovka continued. "Charles Graham and I were partners…and lovers until he betrayed me."

Know thy enemy. If it worked for Sun Tzu… "What happened?"

Madame Petrovka studied her a moment and then leaned back in her chair. "Why not? You actually remind me of myself those many years ago. If you live, this might serve as a cautionary tale of sorts."

Elizabeth tried to ignore the "if you live" part. "You and Graham were on an assignment together?"

"Jack the Ripper," she said with a disquieting smile. "It was quite the plum. It was going incredibly well until I made two mistakes. The first was that I stupidly lost the watch and that led to my second mistake, trusting that as long as Charles had his, it wouldn't matter."

"He left you behind?"

"We'd gotten separated right before the eclipse, but he could have stayed. He could have looked for me. But he… he just left me there. Left me there to rot."

Madame Petrovka took a sip of tea and narrowed her eyes. "Do you know what 1888 London was like for a woman alone, with no money, no connections?"

"I can imagine."

"Not even in your worst nightmares can you imagine it. I was sent to Bedlam. Have you heard of it?"

Elizabeth nodded. She'd heard horror stories about it. About the barbaric treatments they'd used on the patients.

"I spent twelve years there. Twelve. Years. They did unspeakable things in the beginning. Anyone who wasn't mad when they arrived was surely mad when they left. If they left. I found my own way out."

It was all starting to make sense now. She couldn't get her revenge against Charles Graham, but she could on Victor Graham.

Madame Petrovka took a sip of her tea. "It took years to cultivate my new life. But coming from the future does have its advantages. A few months ago I read about Victor Graham and the rest as they say is history."

Elizabeth felt a flash of pity for the woman, but tamped it down quickly. "I'm sorry for what happened to you, but this won't change anything. Victor and Mary Graham didn't do anything to you."

"They had a son, who had a son, who had a son."

"But murder and torture," Elizabeth said. "That's evil. You're not evil."

"No?" she said as she set down her teacup and leaned back in her chair. "You know, most people think evil is something abstracted from man. A demon that crawls out of a pit and takes over some poor man's soul. They think demons are drawn to places like Bedlam. And, oh yes, they're quite real, but demons aren't drawn to places like Bedlam. They're forged there. They're created out of the screams and the agony and the hopelessness. Evil is truly man-made."

That was a frightening concept and one that Elizabeth didn't dare think about right now. She needed to stay focused. On Mary. On Simon. Why hadn't Madame Petrovka simply killed Mary Graham? Assuming she was actually alive. Was she keeping her alive as some sort of bargaining chip? And that's when she realized what the price for Mary Graham was going to be.

"You want the watch."

Madame Petrovka's eyes fluttered. "I do."

Handing over a time travel device to an insane murderer was generally not a good idea unless you didn't have any other ideas. "And you'll give me Mary Graham, unharmed, in exchange?"

"You have my word."

For all that was worth. It was a deal with the Devil, but it was the only deal on the table. And maybe, just maybe, Elizabeth had a trick or two up her own sleeve. "Agreed. But, there are some things I have to take care of first. I'll need some time."

Elizabeth racked her brain for a good meeting place. The middle of the Golden Gate Bridge would have been dramatic, but also stupid considering it wouldn't be built for another thirty years. She wished she'd done more research into the city before she'd come. While the bridge wouldn't do, Golden Gate Park would. Open spaces, if they had to ride out the earthquake, and it looked like they would, that was probably their best bet.

"We'll meet later," Elizabeth said, "At the Temple of Music."

"Good, when?"

She was anxious; that was good. "Five."

"This evening?"

"No," Elizabeth said and knew this part was going to be a tough sell, but she didn't have any choice. "In the morning."

Madame Petrovka shook her head. "Minutes before the earthquake? That's impossible."

"So is time travel," Elizabeth said. "Without a watch."

Chapter Twenty-Four

E LIZABETH PICKED AT HER sandwich and pushed it away. She walked over to the fireplace and stared into the flames. All she could do now was wait. And it blew. Teddy was still hard at work on her second project for him and there wasn't anything she could do to help. The police had accepted their last bribe and she couldn't even get in to see Simon again.

She chewed on what was left of her fingernails and wondered if she'd made the right choices. Her conversation with Travers came back to her with stark clarity. Time was changing and now she was beginning to wonder if, ultimately, she was the one responsible.

It was bad enough that she'd given Teddy the idea for the watches in the first place, now she'd given him an actual watch. Was she responsible for the birth of the Council or would tomorrow show she was responsible for its end?

Mucking with History: My True Story.

Or was it something worse than that? Simon had never believed what Travers had told her. And more and more it looked like he'd been right.

"Idiot!" She pounded her fist down onto the mantle and spun around.

She really needed to stop trusting people so blindly. She wasn't a child, she needed to stop acting like one. What if everything that had happened was all part of some Council plan and she was just a willing pawn in all of it?

The more she thought about it the angrier she got. Angry with the Council for lying to her. No matter what happened, they'd lied by omission at the very least. She'd been fool enough to leap before looking. Simon was here and in prison, all because of her, and unless her half-baked plan worked, she might never see him again. The thought made her truly ill.

A soft knock on the door brought her back to the present. Mrs. Eldridge poked her inside. "Are you all right, dear?"

"I'm fine."

It was clear she wasn't and Mrs. Eldridge nodded toward her uneaten sandwich. "You really should eat something. Can't save the world on an empty stomach, now can you?"

Elizabeth took the older woman's hand and drew strength from her. The hand in hers was fragile, but the woman wasn't. She could only imagine the things Mrs. Eldridge had been through in her life and, yet, she was kind and gentle.

"I'm not very good at waiting."

"No one really is," Mrs. Eldridge said patting hand. "Some of us are just better at pretending we are."

Simon waited at least a half hour after the last guard had appeared before he set to his task. The light in the cell was dim, but his eyes had adjusted well and he sat down on his bunk and began to unwrap his package.

The odor was quite pungent and smelled a bit like a moldy, stale room full of dirty socks. And yet, if you could look past the smell, the cheese was really rather good.

Simon picked up the round and felt the ridge of the cuts to the bottom of the rind. Carefully, he popped the bottom out. Embedded inside were four small colored vials and a tiny note that read: *Red, then blue. Don't touch. xoxo*

He held the vials carefully. They were tiny. The acid or whatever it was inside them must be incredibly aggressive for such a small quantity to be able to burn through iron. With great care, Simon put two of the four vials, one red and one blue, back into their hollows in the cheese. He'd initially thought using the cheese was a bit ridiculous, but not only had the odor frightened off any inspection of the package, the cheese itself was a perfect container to cushion and protect the fragile vials.

He walked to his cell door and felt the plates that covered the lock. The iron was cold and quite substantial under his fingers. He looked down at the two small vials in his hand and knew it was time.

Very carefully, he broke the tip off the red vial. Sure to keep it upright, he reached through the bars. He had to move slowly or he might spill or, worse yet, drop the vial. It was awkward, but he felt the panel of the lock with his free fingers and then tipped the contents of the vial into the keyhole. He repeated the same process with the blue vial and waited.

Nothing happened. Of course. Why should anything be that simple.

Simon was about to reach for the second set of vials when an incredibly acrid smoke began to filter up from the lock casing and then the entire thing burst into a flash of sparks like thermite eating through metal. The fire burned itself out almost as quickly as it had begun.

Simon approached the cell door cautiously. The area where the lock had been was mottled with sizzling holes. He pushed on the bars above it and the door swung open.

"Brilliant."

He grabbed the other two vials and hurried across the office to the filing cabinet, but it was locked. Thank heaven he had two sets of acid. It would take something just that strong to open it.

Simon broke the tip of the first vial and was just about to pour it into the keyhole on the cabinet when a voice behind him said, "How did you do that?"

Simon jumped and nearly dropped the vial, but managed to keep it from slipping from his fingers. Barely. He spun around and didn't see anyone at first. And then he saw a figure emerge from the darkness of the adjoining cell. The man wrapped his hands around the iron bars and pressed his face between them. "Can you help me?"

Olaf Karlsson.

"How long have you been there?" Simon asked. They'd last seen him on the streets in front of the Palace hotel where he'd helped them escape the mob.

Olaf shook his head. "It is all blurry. My head is not well."

No, Simon thought, probably not. Olaf had taken a good crack to skull that day. And now he was here, stuck in this death-trap because of it. Of course, he might have been arrested anyway. It wasn't their fault he was here, was it?

Simon couldn't afford to stand there and chat. Who knew when the guards might decide to check on them? He had to move. He had to get the watch and go.

Simon turned away from Olaf and faced the cabinet. He was just about to use the first vial, but his hand wouldn't move. This time the little voice in his head wasn't Elizabeth's; it was his own.

"Damnit," Simon whispered to the darkness. He couldn't do it.

With a loud grunt, he stormed over to Olaf. "Stand back."

Olaf did as he was told and Simon poured the first and then the second vial into the lock. The iron burned away just as the first had and Simon pulled open the cell door.

Olaf stared at the hole in the iron where the lock had been in disbelief and stuck out his hand to Simon. "Thank you."

Simon shook it quickly. "We need to go. Quietly."

Simon cast one last glance at the filing cabinet. He hated leaving the watch behind, but at least Elizabeth had hers. There was nothing to be done for it anyway. He couldn't break into the cabinet now without trying to smash it to bits. But that would have taken too long and been far too loud. If only it hadn't been his grandfather's.

"Come." Olaf had opened the door and was poking his head outside. "It is clear."

The side door was just where Elizabeth had said it would be and Simon and Olaf slipped out of the building unseen.

Elizabeth was there, waiting for him, just as she'd promised. He smiled in greeting and she threw her arms around his neck and kissed him. "All right?"

"I'm fine."

"Thank you," Olaf said.

Elizabeth pulled back startled. "Where'd he come from? Where'd you come from?"

Simon interrupted her. They had to get as far away from City Hall as they could. "I'll explain it to you later. We need to go."

Elizabeth nodded. "Sorry. My first jailbreak. Got excited."

"Of course," Simon said.

She turned to Olaf. "I'm sorry about before, Olaf. Please, get your family, if you have one, and get out of town. Tonight. The... the police will come looking for you."

The big man nodded.

"Good luck," Elizabeth said.

"And to you," the big man said before he ran off into the night.

"Leaving, what a good idea," Max said from the shadow of a tall elm tree. "Shall we?"

The trio hurried down the dark, empty streets, up one block and down another until they came to Max's car. It was a miracle the entire city didn't wake when he started the damned thing. But somehow they seemed to have the whole world to themselves. Max put the car in gear and they sped off into the night.

"What are we doing here?" Simon asked as they pulled up in front of Teddy Fiske's house. "We should leave town now. The earthquake can't be more than a few hours away."

"The what?" Max said.

"We'll explain later." Elizabeth would have loved nothing more than to have piled Max's car full of the people she'd grown to love here and get the hell out of Dodge. "We still have a few things to do."

She got out of the car and hurried up the path to Teddy's.

"What's she talking about?" Simon asked as he and Max trailed along behind her.

"I'm just the driver. She's the brains of the outfit."

Knowing it would be left open for her, Elizabeth didn't bother to knock on the front door. She pushed it open and ushered the two men inside. They made their way down the hall past the butler Donald, who was tucked in under an afghan and soundly asleep in his chair.

She led them down the hall to the library and smiled as she heard Simon's intake of breath. "I know," she said. "I want."

She led them over to the bookcase and pressed firmly against *Memoirs of the Twentieth Century* and the wall spun away.

Simon paused at the threshold. "Does he know we're coming?"

"He knows a lot more than that." She and Teddy had talked about more than just how to break Simon out of prison the other night. They were fairly even on the secret swapping scale. He understood just how important what she was doing was and he'd given her permission for Simon and even Max to see his laboratory.

She led them through the hall to the other door and then down the winding staircase.

"Teddy Fiske, you mad genius, you," Max said as they emerged into the lab. He left Simon and Elizabeth to Teddy and wandered around the lab trying to soak it all in.

Teddy, who was sitting on a stool and hunched over a table, turned and smiled sheepishly. "It…it worked?"

Elizabeth took Simon's arm. "Perfectly. And the rest of it? Can you do it?"

"Yes, I think so. I'm guessing on a few things, but this really is a remarkable thing." He turned back to his worktable and Simon's eyes went wide at what he saw. Teddy was working on her watch.

"You do good work," Elizabeth said. "Or you will."

Teddy giggled and started to reattach the case.

"Elizabeth?"

She knew Simon wouldn't be happy about her apparently complete and utter disregard for the timeline. "Try and think of it as a minor spoiler," she said hopefully. "I mean, Teddy would have seen a watch soon anyway when he invented it."

He gave her *that* face; that "we are not amused" face that seemed to come included with every Englishman. "I did what had to be done, Simon. Need I remind you that I couldn't have saved you without Teddy's help."

She knew she had him with that one.

He nodded grudgingly. "Thank you for that, Teddy."

Teddy didn't look up from his work and waved a hand over his shoulder in acknowledgement.

Before Simon could argue further, Elizabeth played her trump card. "A wise man I know once said that we simply have to assume everything we've done is meant to be."

"Sounds like something an idiot would say," Simon grumbled.

"Call it determinism or destiny, if it makes you feel better. I'm calling it saving our butts."

She could see that Simon didn't like it, but he conceded the point. They were too far into it now to back out.

"What's he doing with it?" Simon asked. "It's the only one we have now."

His words hit her like a fist to the solar plexus. The only one?

"What do you mean? Yours is…" and she put it together. "Ooohlaf. You used the second set of compounds on his cell door, didn't you?"

"It seemed like the proper thing to do at the time."

"Proper? Oh, Simon," she said taking hold of his arm. He was such a doodle sometimes.

Simon frowned uncomfortably. "As long as your watch works," he said, "it doesn't really matter."

She felt a sudden rush of swelling panic and the tingle of adrenaline coursing through her system. She hadn't considered that her watch would be their only means of escape. She'd just stupidly assumed that Simon would have his. Now, they were going to be stuck here.

Oddly, the prospect didn't frighten her as much as she thought it would. All she'd wanted since this crazy business had started was to have Simon safe and by her side. If they survived the night and had each other, none of the rest of it mattered. At least, it didn't matter to her.

"It will work, won't it?" Simon asked.

"Oh, it'll work, sort of," she assured him. "But it just won't be working for us."

"What exactly do you mean 'not for us'," Simon said pinching the bridge of his nose. "I think you'd better explain to me what's going on here, Elizabeth. From the beginning."

"Right." She pulled one of the stools out from under the table. "You'll probably want to sit down for this."

Chapter Twenty-Five

MAX PARKED THE CAR on a side street near the park. Elizabeth had trouble letting go of the seat and it wasn't because of Max's driving. As she'd told Simon about her plan, the enormity of what was at stake hit home. Again. Simon's life was still at risk. And so was Mary Graham's and her child's. And Max's.

After Max pulled on the emergency brake, Elizabeth turned to him and said, "You don't have to do this."

He smiled. "I know."

"But you don't even know what this is all about and yet—"

"I like you," he said simply and then cast a glance at Simon and raised an eyebrow. "Both of you."

He opened his car door and stepped out. "I learned a long time ago that life is vastly more interesting when you say yes to it." He smiled that winning smile. "Even when no one asks the question."

"Thank you," Elizabeth said, knowing it was hardly enough to give to someone who was about to risk his life for her.

They made their way across the street and into the grove of trees that lined the edge of the park. It was less than half an hour until the earthquake. The building anticipation was fraying her already well-frayed nerves. She could only hope that Travers had been right about Mrs. Eldridge's house surviving the quake. She'd ordered Teddy to take his butler Donald there and wait until she returned. She wasn't sure if she believed in God or not, but she prayed to whomever might be listening for their safety.

The park was beautiful, but eerie. It was always strange to be somewhere deserted that was usually so filled with life. In that last hour before dawn, it felt as if nature itself knew what was coming and forced itself be still in anticipation. They slipped in and out of the trees, as Max led them toward the Temple of Music.

They emerged from the grove of trees onto the large open music concourse. Several rows of large shade trees lined a wide path that led to the base of the Temple. It was impressive, but not the best place to ride out an earthquake. The Temple, an outdoor music theater, was really an immense marble colonnade. Corinthian columns lined either side of a large inset band-shell, a sort of coffered-arch shaped stage.

Three figures stood at the top of the steps – Madame Petrovka, Stryker and Mary Graham. Elizabeth felt her heart pounding against her ribcage. This was it. She and Simon and Max walked forward. The gravel under their feet seemed absurdly loud in the quiet of the park.

They stopped about ten feet from the bottom of the stairs. Elizabeth's throat was dry and her voice sounded strained. "Are you all right, Mary?"

Mary Graham was visibly shaking, but appeared unharmed. She started to step forward, but Stryker grabbed her arm. "I'm… I'm fine," Mary said.

Madame Petrovka eyed Simon and Max carefully before addressing Elizabeth. "As you can see, I've held up my end of the bargain. Do you have yours?"

Elizabeth pulled the watch from her coat pocket and held it out.

Madame Petrovka nearly reached out, but stopped herself. "Very good," she said breathlessly. "Bring it here."

Simon put a hand on Elizabeth's arm. "Send Mrs. Graham down first."

Madame Petrovka cocked her head to the side and made a show of thinking about it. "I don't think so."

"I'll bring the watch as she comes down," Elizabeth said. "That's SOP for this sort of thing, isn't it?" She held out her hands to show she didn't have any weapons. "No tricks."

Madame Petrovka laughed. "Yes, we don't like tricks, do we?" She nodded to Stryker who started down the steps with Mary Graham.

"Let me go," Simon said as he held out his hand for the watch.

"I can do this," Elizabeth said.

Elizabeth took a deep breath and started toward the steps. There were probably a dozen shallow steps between them. Stryker and Mary were nearing halfway. Elizabeth picked up her skirts, climbed the stairs and met them in the middle.

Mary Graham's eyes were filled with tears and she looked like she might pass out at any moment.

"It'll be all right," Elizabeth said.

Stryker held out one hand, the other still gripped Mary's arm. "The watch?"

Elizabeth held the watch out and waited until Stryker let go of Mary before she dropped it into his hand. He examined the cover quickly. Then, he turned and ran up the steps toward Madame Petrovka. She snatched it out of his hand and held it up to the moonlight.

Elizabeth put her arm around Mary's waist and started down the steps. They were almost halfway down when Madame Petrovka spoke.

"Kill them."

Just as Elizabeth turned she saw Stryker stride forward and pull a gun out of his pocket. Elizabeth shoved Mary toward Max as Simon leapt forward and grabbed Elizabeth's arm, pulling her down to the ground. The gunshot echoed against the band-shell and Elizabeth heard a grunt.

Simon rolled on top of her. Was he hurt? Had he been shot? "Simon?"

Mary Graham screamed and a second shot rang out. But it wasn't like the first. It was louder, and yet, farther away. Elizabeth saw Simon's face above hers. His eyes were clear, worried, but he seemed to be all right. Thank God.

She looked toward the stairs and saw Stryker's hand spasm. The gun slipped out of his fingers and fell onto the steps.

Stryker stood frozen in shock for a split-second before he fell backwards, his head hitting the stone steps with a loud crack.

Simon's hands cupped Elizabeth's cheek. "Are you all right?"

They'd hit the ground so hard it had knocked the wind out of her. All she could do was nod.

Simon hurriedly got up and lunged for Stryker's gun. He stood above Stryker ready to fire when he slowly lowered his arm. He turned back and looked behind them, where the second shot had come from.

"Petrovka," Elizabeth said, gaining her breath again.

Simon ran up the rest of the stairs gun at the ready.

Elizabeth got to her knees and turned toward the woods behind them. In the distance, a dark figure stepped out from behind one of the trees of the colonnade, smoke still curling out from the end of his rifle. She'd know him anywhere.

"Gerald."

She was about to go to him, when she heard mixed in with Mary Graham's sobs, Max's groans. She hurried to them and found Mary Graham kneeling over Max.

"He's been shot," Mary said between tearful sniffles.

Elizabeth saw the blood seeping through Max's shirt. There was a splayed bullet hole in his shirt. Why was it splayed outward? Was he shot in the back? She rolled him onto his side and saw a small hole in his back just beneath his shoulder. Through and through was better. Wasn't it? Or was it the other way around?

"Oh, Max," she said. He shouldn't have come with her. What had she done?

"Told you I'd see this through to the end."

Elizabeth eased his jacket lapel back to see the wound. A dark red circle blossomed near the armhole of his waistcoat. She tried to carefully move his shirt material to the side, but he gasped when she did.

Mary Graham cried louder in response.

Gerald knelt down next to them and laid his large musket down on the ground. "Let me see."

"Tell my Aunt Lillian I love her."

"You can tell her yourself," Gerald said.

Max frowned. "What?"

Gerald pulled a handkerchief out of his pocket and stuffed it under Max's jacket over the wound. "Keep pressure on it," he told Mary. When she didn't respond he took her wrist and placed her hand over the wound.

With the help of his rifle, Gerald stood.

"He's not dying?" Elizabeth asked.

"Not even a little. I'll clean the wound when we get him home," Gerald said and joined Simon at the top of the stairs.

Max lifted his head off the ground. "I'm not? Really?"

Elizabeth couldn't help but laugh and despite the pain, Max grinned.

Mary Graham brushed some dirt off his cheek. "You were very brave."

"I was?" Max said.

Elizabeth left them and started up the stairs toward Simon. She passed Stryker's body. A thick puddle of blood spread out behind his head and a single tear of blood spilled out of the socket where his eye had been. Part of her wanted to look away, but she didn't. She couldn't. It was a sickening thing to see a man die and worse still to be glad of it.

"Gone." She heard Gerald grumble.

Pulling herself away from Stryker, she joined Simon and Gerald at the back edge of the main platform. Both men stood staring out into the darkness.

She touched Gerald's arm and when he turned to look at her, she didn't know what to say. He'd saved all of their lives. She wanted to give him a huge, sloppy hug, but knew he probably wouldn't like it. She tried to resist the urge, but she couldn't and threw her arms around him and squeezed for all she was worth. "Thank you, Gerald. Thank you."

After a moment, she felt him awkwardly pat her back and then clear his throat.

Eventually, she let him go. "That was one heck of a shot."

Gerald allowed himself a small smile, but then turned his attention back to dark woods. Once a soldier always a soldier.

"I still don't like the idea of her out there with a watch," Simon said.

"If Teddy did his job, she's got a one-way ticket."

"Even so," Simon said shaking his head.

"We did what we had to do."

Simon turned to her. "Are you sure you're all right?"

"I'm fine, but I think we should get Max out of this chill."

"What time is it?"

Gerald checked his watch. "Quarter till."

Simon nodded. "We need to get Mary and Max back to Mrs. Eldridge's. It's safe, isn't it?"

Elizabeth nodded. "That's what Travers said."

"It'll have to do. As much as I'd rather not be inside, fissures can open anywhere. Too many unknowns." He held out his hand for Elizabeth to help her down the steps. "I think we'll be safest at the house, but we need to hurry."

Gerald and Simon helped Max to stand.

"Can you walk?" Simon asked.

He nodded. "But I can't drive."

Under Max's tutelage, Simon managed to get the car started and after a few false starts, he got them home.

They arrived at Mrs. Eldridge's with just minutes to spare. Unfortunately, Simon wasn't used to driving a car without power steering or power brakes and he parked the car in Max's usual spot, in the begonias.

Mrs. Eldridge and Teddy ran out to meet them.

"Maxwell!" Mrs. Eldridge said when she saw that he was hurt.

"Just a scratch," he said.

She pursed her lips. "You ruined your best suit."

He grinned. "Good to see you too, Aunt Lillian."

With Mrs. Eldridge on one side and Mary Graham on the other, Max made his way up the front steps and into the house.

Teddy ran to Elizabeth's side. "I wanted to come and help, but Gerald locked me in the bathroom."

"You did help. We couldn't have done it without you."

"Everyone into the main hallway. In the back, away from the chandelier," Simon ordered in a voice that brooked no argument. "Take down all of those paintings and plants. Anything that can fall."

"What's going on?" Mary asked.

"In about one minute we're going to have an earthquake, Mary," Elizabeth said. "A really, really big earthquake. I need you to look after Max, can you do that for me?"

"Yes." They both helped Max down to sit on the floor.

Max grimaced, but didn't seem to be doing to badly. "About that earthquake…"

"I'm afraid, you're just going to have to trust me on this one."

Simon had grabbed cushions from the salon and handed them out. "Get down and cover your heads with these."

Elizabeth had always thought the worst part of an earthquake was the surprise of it. Now, as she waited for one to come, she wasn't so sure.

Teddy and Gerald helped Donald down to the floor. Teddy handed him a pillow and put his arm around the old man.

Gerald helped Mrs. Eldridge to the ground and took her hand. "Just hold onto to me, Lillian."

Just as Simon was coming to Elizabeth, it struck. It started with a deep rumble just like the proverbial freight train. It grew louder and more insistent and then a loud boom ruptured the air and the entire house started to shake. Simon was nearly thrown off his feet. He held on to the wall and struggled to her side. He wrapped his arms around her as they fell to their knees together and held on to each for dear life.

She'd been through a few minor earthquakes before, but never anything like this. It was like a giant had shoved their entire house ten feet and then jerked it back again and then shook it like a baby's rattle. And the sound was deafening. The walls shook and cracked and popped. She could hear cabinets opening, spilling out their contents to the floor and slamming shut again. The chandelier swayed back and forth, nearly touching the ceiling. The crystals clinked against each other and a few fell like icicles to the floor.

Glass shattered and each large jerk came with a horrible booming sound. And beneath it all was a deep, sickening roar. Elizabeth shut her eyes and tried push down the fear and dread in her chest.

She started to feel dizzy when she realized the entire house was rolling. Waves of earth undulated underneath them and then another vicious jolt came and another. What if they'd been wrong? What if the house shook apart around them?

Mary Graham cried out and Elizabeth heard Max telling her it would be all right. It felt like the shaking would never stop. It ebbed and flowed and each peak was more horrible than the last until, finally, the shaking began to slow. And eventually, it ended.

Elizabeth gripped Simon's hand even tighter then, sure the earth was just playing with her and another worse tremor was sure to follow. There was something primal and deeply disturbing about an earthquake, like the planet itself was trying to shrug you off its shoulder. They waited for an anxious minute before believing it was truly over.

"Is everyone all right?" she asked. Frightened murmurs answered her.

Simon helped Elizabeth stand and they took stock of the house. It wasn't badly damaged. At least Travers hadn't lied about that. Some lamps had overturned, books were tossed from their shelves and several of the windows had shattered, but it could have been far worse. And, Elizabeth thought with a sinking feeling. It would be.

Like nearly everywhere else in the city, the survivors stumbled from their houses out into the street. Most people huddled in their nightclothes and chattered anxiously. Nob Hill had been spared the worst of it. Most of the houses were still intact, but she knew that the rest of city lay in ruins. Already, the smoke from dozens of fires filled the morning sky. The worst was yet to come.

Chapter Twenty-Six

SIMON LOOKED DOWN THE block in the direction of City Hall, but he couldn't see much. The penumbral eclipse that would take them home was scheduled to begin in less than an hour. And he had no idea when the next would come. They had to try to get to his watch, which was still locked up in the jail at City Hall, before then.

He came back to Elizabeth's side. "We should go."

"What do you mean?"

"The watch. We have to at least try to retrieve it. It's possible the earthquake destroyed it, but if there's a chance we can return home, Elizabeth, we have to take it."

He could tell from her expression that she knew he was right, but wasn't ready to accept it just yet. Unfortunately, they didn't have the luxury of time just now. When did they ever?

"Max is hurt," Elizabeth said, but Simon could tell even she didn't buy her own excuse.

"The others can take care of him. Elizabeth, we don't belong here. You know that." What he didn't say, couldn't say in front everyone else, was that he wanted to start again with her, to build a new life back home.

Elizabeth looked around at the others. "I just didn't think it would be this hard."

Much to his chagrin, he found himself feeling much the same way. He'd grown surprisingly attached to these people. He hated to press the issue, but they didn't have time to spare. "We need to go. And if the watch has been destroyed you might get your wish anyway."

"That isn't what I'm wishing for," she said. And he could see in her eyes, as difficult as it was, she'd made up her mind.

The group had gathered in Mrs. Eldridge's front yard and Elizabeth plastered on a smile and joined them. "Simon and I have to go."

"No," Teddy said. "So soon?"

"I can't tell you how much each of you means to me."

Her voice was already beginning to quiver dangerously.

"All of you," Simon added. He hated emotional scenes, but Elizabeth needed this. He ignored the fact that he felt a traitorous lump forming in his own throat. He cleared it and let Elizabeth say her goodbyes.

"I don't know what to say," she said. "You all know how I feel about you."

Mrs. Eldridge stepped forward. "We do. And that's more than enough, dear. Another rule to live by: Never say goodbye."

Elizabeth nodded and wiped the tears from her eyes with the back of her hand. "Right."

Teddy looked like he was ready to burst into tears when he suddenly brightened and dug into his jacket pocket. "I almost forgot. I made you something!"

He held out a long silver chain with a small, ornate watch key on the end and dropped it into Elizabeth's outstretched hand.

"What is it?" she asked.

Teddy grinned. "The moon."

Elizabeth had no idea what that meant, but when did she ever know what Teddy really meant? He looked back at her with such joy and sadness, she had to bite her lip to keep from crying. She slipped the chain over her neck and hugged Teddy for all she was worth.

"It's time," Simon said, coming to her side.

She sniffled and nodded.

"Those fires will be coming this way," Simon said to Gerald and Mrs. Eldridge. "You should gather what you can and leave now. I'm afraid nowhere in the city will be safe soon."

Mrs. Eldridge looked down the street and then back to her beautiful house. Gerald put an arm around her shoulders. "We've been through worse, Lillian."

She smiled up at him and nodded.

"You two had better hurry," Gerald said. "That fire's getting closer awfully fast. Be careful."

"We will." Simon put his arm around Elizabeth and eased her away from the house and out into the street. Together they started the long, dangerous journey to City Hall.

He'd seen photographs, of course, but nothing prepared him for the reality of a disaster on a scale like this. Houses leaned against their neighbors, teetering on the edge of collapse. Bottom stories were flattened under the weight of what rested above. Facades had been shorn off completely leaving the rooms inside looking like a child's dollhouse. In many cases, too many, entire buildings were no more than piles of brick and stone.

People wandered aimlessly, lost in a haze of shock and disbelief. A horse-drawn fire truck raced down the street, bell clanging and dog barking. A man clutched a bible to his chest and preached of damnation and salvation. Smoke billowed out of small fires that were soon to grow into flames that would devour what was left of the city.

But the worst of it were the sounds—the thunk of brick hitting brick as someone tried to dig out a loved one from the rubble. The cries of children for their lost parents and the agonizing wail of someone who's just realized they'd lost everyone they loved.

Simon pulled Elizabeth more tightly to his side. If emotions were colors, this world would have been black. There was so much pain and agony in the air that every breath made him sick to his stomach. He knew that the initial shock, the numbness that comes from a sharp blow, would soon fade. He prayed they were long gone from this place by then, but the deeper they got into the city, the more difficult it became.

The streets were cluttered with debris and overturned carts. A giant rift had opened in the middle of one street. It was easily four feet wide and God only knows how deep. The fissure made a jagged path down the center of the road and Simon could see part of a cart and a horse's stiff legs sticking up from the hole.

City Hall, or what was left of it, loomed in the distance. The great dome was no more than a framework now, like a giant bird-cage. He felt hope slipping away.

"Help me!" someone cried from the side of the road. "Please!"

It was a young boy, no more than twelve. He stood on top of a pile of rubble and called to them, to anyone for help.

"Simon," Elizabeth said at his side.

He knew there would be hundreds, even thousands of cries like that today. They couldn't help them all.

"Please, my sister's under here!"

But they could help this one. Simon ran to the boy. "Where is she?"

"Under here, I think," the boy said. "But I can't lift it."

Simon and Elizabeth scrambled across the loose stones and saw the large slab of masonry. It must have weighed several hundred pounds.

They tried, but there was no way the three of them could move it. It was far too heavy. Then, he noticed a small hand wedged beneath the stone. He'd had enough of dead children on this trip. This girl would not be another.

He saw a man across the street and called out to him. "You there! Help us!"

Elizabeth ran to the man and practically dragged him back. He had a large gash on his forehead and was covered from head to toe with a fine dust.

"There's a little girl trapped," she said and that seemed to rouse the man. His eyes cleared a little and he climbed up next to Simon.

"On three," Simon said. "One, two, three."

Together they lifted the stone slab and tossed it aside. The boy jumped down into the hole and emerged with a little girl clinging to his side. The other man helped him navigate a path across the debris to the street.

Elizabeth stared after the boy and his sister until Simon took her arm and led her away. He didn't blame her. Any moment of triumph amidst the horror had to be savored. But he couldn't give in to the emotions. If they lingered they'd be swallowed up by the need.

"This way," he said and led them down the side street he recognized from the night of his escape.

It was difficult to tell what had been where. City Hall was a complete ruin. He judged the distance from the street corner and saw the uprooted remains of the large oak Max had been leaning against.

"This is it," he said.

The door he'd escaped through wasn't there anymore. The entire wing looked to have collapsed.

"The blueprints showed that the cell was about 25 feet this way," Elizabeth said as she ran along the edge of the debris.

Simon followed her until she stopped. "Right about here."

"It was in the filing cabinet by the door," Simon said as they both clambered over the stones. Elizabeth kept catching her toe on the hem of her skirts, but he knew better than to tell her to let him do it. They were, after all, partners, in this together.

They tossed stone after stone aside and tried to find where the doorway had been, but it all looked the same now. They dug for what felt like hours, but was only minutes. Time felt like it was stretching out and then contracting. He felt his hope slipping away when Elizabeth called out to him.

"Over here!"

He picked his way over to her and looked where she was pointing. Something metal caught the light. He moved more stones and saw that it was one of the brass plates on the front of the cabinet.

It took all the strength either of them had left to move some of the large stones. Somehow, the cabinet hadn't been completely crushed by the weight of the ceiling collapsing on top of it. Through the hole they'd dug Simon could see that the top drawer had been split open. Please let the watch be all right, he thought, as he lay down on top of the rubble and reached down into the hole.

He felt his way around the inside of the drawer and his fingers brushed against something smooth and metal. He strained against the rocks, forcing his arm further into the hole. He felt the edges of the watch and wrapped his fingers around it and pulled it out in triumph.

He handed Elizabeth the watch and reached into the hole again. He grabbed on to the small jewelry box and stuffed it into his jacket pocket. They made their way out of the rubble and onto the grass. The world around them was still in chaos. Bells clanged in the distance, men shouted and bits of building continued to crumble.

Elizabeth ran her fingers over a large dent in the watchcase. "Do you think it'll still work?"

"Open it."

The watch hands still turned and the small moon inset was sliding to a new phase. But there was no way to tell if the watch would still take them home.

"I'm sorry," she said.

He tilted her head up, surprised to find tears in her eyes. "Whatever for?"

"This is all my fault. I believed the Council even when you told me not to. They could have made up any old story and I would have bought it hook, line and sinker. I'm a schlemiel."

"Don't be ridiculous," he said wiping a tear from her cheek with the pad of his thumb. "Everything you did, you did out of love. Don't you think I know that? Don't you think I love you all the more for it?"

"What if we never get home?"

"Whatever happens, Elizabeth, I don't regret one moment I've spent with you."

He leaned down to kiss her and just as their lips met, the paralyzing, electric blue light snaked up from the watch and engulfed them both. And sent them home.

She was finally free. Her head was swimming, but she was free. Something was wrong though. She hadn't expected it to be dark. Why did she taste soot in the night air?

Someone bumped into her from behind and she nearly dropped the watch. Finally, her head began to clear.

The clatter of hooves on cobblestones made her turn her head and she saw someone jump into the back of a carriage.

No.

She started to run, but a strong arm grabbed her. "That's as far as you go."

She spun around to see a guard from the hospital and then another.

"Don't know where you got those clothes, but they're the last taste of freedom you'll ever have."

Another man gripped her arm painfully and she felt the cold of the iron manacles as they clamped tightly around her wrists and the watch was ripped from her hand.

"No," she mumbled. It couldn't be. It couldn't be. "I can't go back."

The guards spun her around and led her away from the gate. Led her back to the hospital. Back to Bedlam.

THE END

ABOUT THE AUTHOR

MONIQUE WAS BORN IN Houston, Texas, but her family soon moved to Southern California. She grew up on both coasts, living in Connecticut and California. She currently resides in Southern California with her naughty Siamese cat, Monkey.

Monique attended the University of Southern California's Film School where she earned a BFA from the Filmic Writing department. Monique worked in television for several years before joining the family business. She now works full-time as a freelance writer and novelist. Her novels *Out of Time* and *When the Walls Fell* are the first two books in the *Out of Time* series.

She's currently working on an adaptation of one of her screenplays, her father's memoirs about his time in the Air Force's Air Rescue Service and the third book in the *Out of Time* series.

For news and information about Monique and upcoming releases, please visit: http://moniquemartin.weebly.com/

Follow Monique on Twitter: http://twitter.com/ - !/_MoniqueMartin_

Like Monique on Facebook: https://www.facebook.com/pages/Monique-Martin-Author/132268193491541

An Excerpt From

Out Of Time

The first book of the "Out of Time" series by Monique Martin

CHAPTER ONE

THE NIGHTMARES HAD COME again.

Simon Cross pushed himself off the bed and away from the cold, sweat-soaked sheets. His heart racing, his breath quick and rough, he forced his eyes to adjust to the dark room as the last vestiges of sleep faded.

He glared down at his bed, as if it were to blame, as if the sheets and pillows had knowingly harbored the nightmare. He felt a surge of panic and escaped from the darkened bedroom.

The moon was nearly full and cast its silvery light through the open curtains giving the living room an unearthly glow. Vague shadows stretched out like the taunting specters of his nightmare. Ignoring everything but his destination, he strode to the liquor cabinet. His hands trembled as he poured a stiff Scotch and downed it in one swig. Without pause, he poured another. His hands gripped the crystal glass as he tried in vain to keep it from clattering on the silver tray.

Disgusted with his weakness, he slammed the bottle down and clamped his eyes shut. His hands still trembled.

"Bloody hell."

The last time he'd had a nightmare like this was over thirty years ago. Yet, the memory rang with sharp clarity in his mind. His grandfather. The violence. The blood. And above all, the helplessness.

Simon let out a short burst of breath. He tried to convince himself this had merely been another dream. Another dream about her.

Ignoring the stacks of open boxes littering the floor, he tightened his jaw, grabbed the glass of Scotch and prowled across the room. He'd dreamt of her before. He was, after all, only human. She was attractive, intelligent and everything he wanted, but could never have. It was only natural she'd be in his thoughts. But there was nothing natural about this dream. This nightmare. This wasn't a fool's late night fantasy, brought on by loneliness and assuaged by a cold shower. This was something unspeakable.

Unconsciously, he clenched and unclenched his free hand. No concrete images remained, just an unwavering sense of horror, of an inevitable evil.

Exactly as it had been before.

He took another drink and concentrated on the warm burning sensation as the liquor seeped down into his chest. There was no avoiding the harbinger of his dream. With the certainty only a condemned man can feel, he knew one absolute truth.

Elizabeth West was going to die.

Elizabeth had heard it all before. But no matter how many times she listened to Professor Cross' lectures, she marveled at the way he held the class in the palm of his hand. As always, there wasn't an empty seat in the classroom. Introduction to Occult Studies was a favorite at the University of California Santa Barbara. Most students were there for the excitement of it, the dark abiding thrill of all things supernatural, like attending a semester-long horror movie. A few, like herself, were there for something more.

When she'd taken his class as an undergraduate, floating along in the sea of the undeclared, she had no idea that four years later she'd be his graduate teaching assistant working toward her Masters in Occult Studies. A meandering path through her Humanities requirements had left her still wanting for something. While all the courses were interesting, none of them sparked her interest. Until she happened upon Professor Cross' class.

In retrospect, she wasn't sure if it was the man or the subject that had first drawn her in, and in the end it didn't matter. It had taken persistence and a thick skin to convince him she was serious about becoming his graduate teaching assistant. At first, she didn't understand why he'd tried to dissuade her. After attending one Board of Chancellors' meeting in his stead, she had a pretty good idea. Occult Studies was nothing more than a curiosity in their eyes. The poor foster child of interdepartmental parents, Occult Studies was hardly recognized as a serious area of academia. Technically it fell under the auspices of Folklore and Mythology, but for Professor Cross it was a life's work and something very real. His passion inspired her, in more ways than one.

Elizabeth watched him pace slowly behind the lectern, hypnotizing the class with his fluid movements, setting them up for the kill. His keen eyes scanned the classroom, pulling each student under his spell. When his eyes fell upon her, he paused, almost losing his place. He frowned and continued. No one else noticed the minor lapse, but claxons went off in Elizabeth's mind.

There was something off about him today. His normally squared shoulders were hunched. His sandy brown hair was slightly unkempt as though he'd dragged his fingers through it too many times. She'd noticed that morning he seemed out of sorts, and chalked it up to overwork. But there really wasn't a time when Professor Cross wasn't overworked. Something was definitely wrong. The untrained eye would see only typical Cross—brilliant, terse and otherwise occupied. Elizabeth knew him far too well to believe the simplicity of his façade. Working in close quarters had given her insights into the man that most people never knew. What others saw as detachment, she saw as stoic vulnerability.

On the rare occasion he'd let his guard down, she'd seen the depths of the man inside. She knew nothing could ever come of it. Aside from the twenty year age difference, he listened to Stravinsky, she listened to Sting. He was from South of London, she was from North of Lubbock. He grew up with a silver spoon, she grew up with a spork. It was hopeless. She was used to dreaming about things she could never have. There was no reason to think this was anything different.

Simon walked across the stage, powerfully graceful and deceptively smooth. Elizabeth shifted in her seat and needlessly adjusted her skirt.

Why did he have to be so damn attractive? He was handsome. The overwhelming female enrollment in his class was testimony to that. Tall, a few inches over six feet, slender, but not lanky. Eyes of a deep green, tinged with the sadness of having seen too much of the world. And his voice—a hypnotic, deep baritone with a cut glass English accent. But those weren't the things she'd fallen in love with. It was something else, something gentle beneath the hard edge, something needful beneath the control.

"And unlike the overly sentimentalized versions of vampires we see in today's media," Professor Cross said, his voice dripping with sarcasm. "Calmet's writings spoke to the truth of the beast. An unyielding malevolence." He paused and leaned on the podium. "Purge Tom Cruise from your malleable little minds."

The class snickered, and he waited impatiently for them to settle. "The vampire would suck the blood of the living, so as to make the victim's body fall away visibly to skin and bones. An insatiable hunger that kills without remorse," he said and surveyed the classroom.

Elizabeth knew that look, a forlorn hope of seeing some spark of interest, or God forbid, hear some intelligent discourse on the subject. Instead, a blonde girl sitting in the back row made a sound of disgust.

Professor Cross frowned. "Must you do that every class, Miss Danzler?"

She had the good sense to look chagrined. "Sorry, Professor."

Before he could retort that perhaps she should consider a field of study other than the occult, as Elizabeth knew he would, a handsome, athletic student sitting next to her bared his biceps and chimed in, "Don't worry, baby. These are lethal in all dimensions."

Professor Cross assumed his well-practiced air of indifference. "Failing that, Mr. Andrews, you could always bludgeon the demon to death with your monumental ego."

A wave of stifled laughter traveled across the room. As much as the students enjoyed the dark fascination of Cross' Occult Studies course, they also loved his unrelenting sarcasm. Sometimes, he went too far of course, and Elizabeth was left to smooth down the ruffled feathers.

"Sadly, it appears the only thing thicker than your muscles is your skull."

This was one of those times.

The class ended and the students began to pack up. "Don't forget chapters seventeen and eighteen of Grey's *Lycanthropy of Eastern Europe* for next week."

Elizabeth left her seat and started toward the back of the classroom. Time for a little damage control.

Professor Cross gathered his notes from the podium and turned to look for his assistant. Miss West had already left her customary front row seat and was climbing the stairs toward the back of the amphitheater.

Simon closed his briefcase with more force than necessary and tried to look away. He frowned at the familiar way Elizabeth touched the young man's forearm. Not that he was jealous. That would be patently absurd. Simon simply didn't suffer fools gladly, even by proxy. His mood soured as Elizabeth said something undoubtedly utterly charming and won a laugh from the hulking imbecile. Simon gritted his teeth and waited impatiently for the scene to come to an end. Elizabeth smiled one last time and headed back down the stairs. He glared at her in greeting and gestured brusquely that they should leave.

His mood still sour, Simon opened the classroom door and held it for her. Elizabeth smiled her thanks and walked out into the corridor. He followed her out, moving quickly down the crowded hall, keeping his strides long, forcing her to almost jog to keep up. After a few moments of tense silence, he stopped abruptly and turned to glare down at her.

"I don't need a nursemaid, Miss West."

Elizabeth cocked her head to the side and frowned. "That's debatable, but I wasn't—"

Simon arched an eyebrow in disbelief, challenging her to deny it.

"All right, I was."

Simon snorted.

"But you've got to admit you were in rare form, even for you."

"Your point?"

"That a little browbeating goes a long way. Lance is a good guy. He was just showing off."

"For your benefit, I suppose?" Simon said and instantly wished he could take the words back.

Elizabeth laughed. "Hardly. I'm not exactly his type," she said with a rueful, lopsided smile.

He felt an odd urge to comfort her, to tell her Andrews was a simpleton, but the words died in his throat. How did she do that? One moment she was forthright and confident, challenging him; and the next shy and achingly vulnerable.

"Besides," she added. "It'd be unethical to date a student."

That was something he'd told himself daily. He cleared his throat uncomfortably. "Yes, quite right. Well, we have work to do. Shall we?" he said and gestured down the hall.

"No rest for the wicked," she said with a grin and started down the corridor.

Simon watched her disappear into the mass of students and took a deep breath. The scent of her perfume lingered in the air. "None indeed."

Elizabeth set down her pen and massaged her cramping fingers. She could swear she did more work correcting the papers than the students did writing them. And the tiny desk lamp that passed for light in the room was making her eyes cross.

It had taken Professor Cross a year to acquiesce to her request for an actual desk in his office. At first, he'd done everything he could to keep her out of what she liked to call his inner sanctum. He kept the room dark. Suitable, he'd said, for their work. The room was tiny, another testament to the lack of enthusiasm on the part of the Board. He'd been a professor there for nearly ten years and had labored in obscurity. Although, he seemed just as pleased that they left him alone.

Grant money was scarce, if not non-existent, and so he used his own money to further their research. For all the good it did. It seemed the latest get rich quick scheme in the former Soviet Union was the illegal export of so-called occult artifacts—a lock of genuine Baba Yaga hair or, her personal favorite, werewolf droppings. Capitalism at its best. For all the money spent, not one thing had been authentic. But Professor Cross was undeterred, and so their research trudged on.

Elizabeth rubbed her eyes and stole a glimpse of him in the reflection of the glass covering the Bosch print on the wall, the only decoration in an otherwise impersonal office. He really did look tired. More than that, he looked worried. Bent over his desk, one hand wrapped around his head casting a shadow over his face.

"You look like hell," she said.

Simon's eyes snapped up to meet hers. "Thank you," he said tartly.

"I just meant… Are you all right?"

Elizabeth steeled herself for his curt reply, but something stopped him. He looked at her and the hard light in his green eyes softened. "I'm fine," he said. "Thank you."

Then, as quickly as it had disappeared, his natural aloofness re-established itself. He indicated the large stack of graded papers on his desk. "I think that's enough for one night."

Elizabeth shook her head. "I'm okay."

"You can finish the rest tomorrow and drop them off at my house."

A yawn squelched any protest she was going to make. "All right. I could use some good sleep for a change. I've been having this dream. Very David Lynch. Totally and completely unnerving."

Simon dropped his pen and quickly retrieved it. "I see."

Elizabeth shrugged and packed her bag. "I'm gonna sleep like the dead tonight."

She turned back to say goodnight and found him staring at her again with the oddest expression on his face. "Are you sure you're okay?"

He seemed to come back to himself. "Yes, of course. Goodnight, Miss West."

"Good night, Professor," she said and left the office, her footfalls echoing down the empty hallway.

Simon gripped his pen so tightly his knuckles were white with the strain. The mention of her dream brought back the memory of his nightmare from the last few nights. He'd wanted desperately to ask her about her dream, to tell her about his, but felt too foolish. What could he say? I dreamt about you last night. Don't know any details, but you died a horrible death. Have a good night. Pillock.

He forced himself to put down his pen and pushed away the fresh wave of anxiety that threatened to pull him under. He'd managed for most of the day to forget, to feel safe in having her by his side. He couldn't say anything, but he couldn't let her walk away either. Before he knew it, he was on his feet and hurrying out into the hall. She was nearly at the corner when he caught her. "May I walk you to your car?"

Elizabeth started and then blinked at him in surprise. "I'm right outside," she said pointing to the doorway around the bend. "It's not really far enough for a walking to."

He hadn't expected her to refuse and felt like a schoolboy who'd been turned down for a date. "Yes, well then. Good night, Miss West," he said and turned back toward his office before he could make a bigger fool of himself. He walked into his office and closed the door. The main door to the building closed with a thud, and he put his hand to his forehead. Gibbering dolt. Tongue-tied over a woman half his age.

Moments later, he heard voices outside and looked out his office window. Elizabeth waved goodbye to someone then walked alone into the parking lot.

He watched her through the slats of the louvered blinds. He was used to being on the inside looking out. It was how he lived. The loneliness had become a welcome companion, reinforcing old memories and keeping him safe from new ones.

He scanned the darkness for unseen dangers, but the night was quiet and still. Elizabeth made her way to her decrepit VW Bug and unlocked it. She opened the door, but didn't get in. She paused and lifted her head as if she'd heard something. Simon felt his heart lurch. He strained to see the threat, ready to go to her. After a painfully long moment, she shook her head and got into the car.

Simon let out a breath he didn't know he'd been holding and watched her pull out of the lot. He stood at the window long after the red of her tail lights had been swallowed by the night. What was it about that woman that left him feeling so undone? He was a solitary man, by choice and by circumstance. He'd grown used to living according to his own whim and no one else's. Then Elizabeth West had come into his life. She was curious, honest, unafraid and completely maddening. He had managed perfectly well without her and yet, he couldn't quite remember how.

Made in the USA
San Bernardino, CA
08 May 2015